KV-703-753

EAST OF SUEZ

THE STORY:

In Suez town Jonathan Samways, ship's apprentice, stumbled across a man who had been attacked and fatally injured by gangsters. He gave Jonathan a scrap of paper which told of a treasure that the dying man, known as the Red Cormorant, had hidden.

Jonathan escaped the scene only with difficulty, and on arriving in England he and his father, a famous former officer of the Palestine Police, were all but killed by the gang, who, later, pursued him on his treasure hunt to Palestine. He faced many perils by sea and land. He was caught in a great hurricane aboard a small boat and was hunted over the mountains of the Holy Land by both Israel and Arab troops as well as by brigands and guerrillas.

This latest stirring tale of modern adventure by an author who knows the Near East intimately, vividly portrays what life is like today along the newest and most romantic borderland in the world—where the new State of Israel marches with the Arab Kingdom.

Frontispiece

"He realized that this must be the craft which had destroyed his little ship."

EAST OF SUEZ

By

DOUGLAS V. DUFF

HERBERT JENKINS LIMITED

First Published by
Herbert Jenkins Ltd.
3 *Duke of York Street*
London S.W. 1
1950

Printed by C. *Tinling & Co.* Ltd., *Liverpool, London and Prescot*

CONTENTS

LIST OF ILLUSTRATIONS

CHAPTER 1

THE RED CORMORANT

JONATHAN SAMWAYS, third-year cadet aboard the Red Diamond cargo-liner *Symondsbury Mote*, thought his luck was really in when the 10,000 ton ship developed engine-trouble and had to enter Suez docks for repairs. He was the only person aboard who did so, for anywhere more unlovely than the sweltering port at the head of the Red Sea in late July, it is difficult to imagine. The reason for his pleasure at this unexpected event was that Jonathan had been brought up differently from most British lads.

His father, a widower, was a District Superintendent of Palestine Police in the old days when Britain ruled the Holy Land, so that his son had grown up in the barracks of the Arab troops whom his father had commanded. Jonathan spoke both Arabic and Hebrew as well as he did English, and, although he went to a school in England when he was twelve, he had never lost contact with the land of his birth for as he had few relatives in Britain the motherless lad always returned to Palestine for his holidays.

His original ambition had been to follow his father into the commissioned ranks of the Palestine

Police, but, before he was old enough to be given his appointment as a cadet, the British Mandate ended and the old Force was disbanded. As none of the other Colonial Constabularies appealed to him he signed his indentures as an apprentice in the Red Diamond Line, so that as he entered Suez Docks he was only six months off the day when he would possess sufficient sea-service to sit for his examination as Second Mate in the Merchant Navy.

One reason why he was so pleased to be staying a few days in Suez was that he would have a chance to speak his beloved Arabic, even though the Egyptian accent is harsh and hard compared to the beautiful *Shami*, the Damascus dialect of Palestine, called by the Arabs " The Tongue of the Angels of Allah." An even greater satisfaction was that Mustafa Effendi el Lahami lived in Suez town, where he had settled down as shop-keeper after being pensioned from the Palestine Police. Mustafa Effendi was one of those gallant Egyptians who first entered the Holy Land in 1917 as part of Lord Allenby's conquering armies, and who had remained there in the British service until the ending of the Mandate. He had been Colonel Samways' senior Local Officer for several years, and taught Jonathan all he knew of horsemastership and many other useful accomplishments such as the ability to use and maintain a large variety of weapons.

Jonathan had been visiting his old friend and teacher on that third night of the ship's stay. He had come to the town from the docks in Port Tewfik in a taxi which had carried him along the long narrow causeway which connects that settlement with the ancient city of Suez. Mustafa Effendi, delighted to entertain his old colonel's son, had put on a big show, so that most of his part of Suez knew who Jonathan was, and why he was visiting the prosperous gunsmith. There had been singing and dancing and Mustafa Effendi's other guests had been more than pleased when they discovered the fluency and the purity of the lad's Arabic, together with his understanding of their ways of thought, so that altogether it had been a really enjoyable party.

There happened to be no taxi available when Jonathan left the hospitable armourer's house at about quarter-past eleven, and as he was due back aboard by midnight he dared not wait on the off-chance that one could be found. Mr. Chalmers, the Chief Officer, was extremely strict about his three cadets returning from leave on time and Jonathan knew he would take no excuses for tardiness. Jonathan, dreading to be late, decided to walk back to the ship ; it was not more than a couple of miles from Mustafa Effendi's house in any case and most of it was along the narrow causeway.

No greater contrast than that between the

ancient, typically Levantine town of Suez, with its tall, crumbling buildings, narrow streets and its rabbit warren of humanity living in crowded tenements and the modern, European-style villa-houses of its satellite, Port Tewfik, can be imagined. Suez has been a port, and an inhabited town, ever since the dawn of History, but Port Tewfik only came into existence with the opening of the great Canal. It is sited on an artificial island, mainly composed of clay excavated from the Canal, or sand dredged from its approaches, and its only rail and road connection is by way of the narrow causeway which runs direct to Suez. Port Tewfik houses are mainly of the French Mediterranean type, clean, red-tiled villas standing in their own gardens of bougainvillea and scarlet hibiscus, while the only sign of real commercial activity are its docks on the western side of the causeway's junction with the island.

The streets between the tall, crumbling tenements were foul and very hot with the latent heat the sun had baked into them during the long and burning day, and which was swamping back into the cooler night air. Jonathan saw few pedestrians, in fact the streets were almost deserted except for one patrol of white-duck uniformed policemen, who, incongruously enough, were wearing British-style shrapnel-helmets and carrying shot-guns, for Suez can be a very dangerous place for wayfarers and patrolling constables once late night has come.

He pressed ahead with the perspiration streaming down his body, for the stifling airlessness of the heat between the houses was almost too great to be borne even by anyone wearing white tropical uniform. His need to hurry if he was to return to *Symondsbury Mote* in time to avoid a humiliating interview with the Chief Officer in the morning, which might entail the stoppage of all further shore-leave, made matters all the worse, and caused him to be less wary than he should have been in such a dangerous neighbourhood.

He saw nothing suspicious, and certainly heard no sounds that he could have considered sinister when, on rounding one of the last corners before stepping on to the causeway, two human bodies hurtled round it, and cannoned into him so violently that he was flung flat on his back. Jonathan was so completely astonished that he did not even see the knife which the first man hurled at him, but he felt the burning pain of its sharp tip as it ripped the side of his white duck tunic and scratched a shallow furrow along his ribs.

For one terrible second he thought he was finished ! With the agonising feeling that he would become just one more of the many corpses of sailormen who have been picked up in the gutters of Levantine towns, he staggered upright and struck out wildly, his fist crashing into a smooth face. He lashed out simultaneously with his foot and sent the light buckskin shoe he was wearing into another body. In an instant his assailants were on their feet again but before he could make any outcry, he saw their two forms darting away in the light of the distant street-lamps until they disappeared down an alleyway leading to the canal banks, the most notorious slum of the ancient and evil town.

He knew that it was useless to shout for help, even though he could feel a slight trickle of something warm running down his side, and looking in that direction, saw a dark stain spreading on the whiteness of his jacket. If he did shout he might, indeed, bring the police, but they would take him to the barracks to make a statement, and that would keep him away from his ship for hours. If he was more than a few minutes late Mr. Chalmers would be telephoning the British Consul and every other authority in the area, kicking up an awful fuss about his missing cadet, and Jonathan knew that if that was once allowed to happen, no excuse on his part would win him any further shore-leave. No, he told himself, if he wanted to visit Mustafa Effendi again he had best forget what had happened and hurry back to Port Tewfik.

While he was reassuring himself that the wound was a mere scratch that could be attended to by using a little iodine as soon as he got aboard, he heard a deep groan behind, followed by a sound as though someone was blowing bubbles with his face under water. It came from the dark shadows just down the alley at whose head he was standing ; those murdering swine who had attacked him must have been stooping over their victim when Jonathan's arrival had disturbed them and sent them flapping away like crows frightened from their carrion. All of a sudden he felt violently sick as the thought of what he had escaped struck fully home ; those assassins had not been play-acting—it was only by the mercy of God that he, too, was not lying on the dusty pavement coughing out his life, like some poor fellow was doing down in the darkness of the alley.

Jonathan's instincts to help the stricken man took him into the darkness without any thoughts that yet another murderer might still be lurking in the deep shadows. Fortunately there was no one there and, as he knelt beside the body of a man whom he found lying in the middle of the narrow lane, Jonathan saw he was dressed in the mixture of cast-off tropical uniforms and sacking that one so often sees worn by longshoremen and stevedores in Egyptian ports. To the lad's surprise, however, the wounded man was murmuring in German. Semi-distinct references to his mother, to his boyhood home and to other long-remembered things were pouring in a gentle, whispering spate from his tortured lips.

" Hold up," Jonathan said soothingly. " Let

me see if I can help you," and involuntarily he spoke in English.

The sound of his voice brought the dying man to his senses.

" Ein Engländer," he muttered. " An Englishman, and a naval officer," he went on, not able to distinguish Jonathan's Red Diamond cap-badge and buttons from those of a Royal Naval officer in such desperate surroundings. " *Gott sei dank.* It is better than nothing. Who are you ? " he asked, a flare-up of strength taking the place of the awful bubbling which had been going on ever since Jonathan reached him.

" I am English," the lad admitted. " My name is Jonathan Samways and I belong to the *Symondsbury Mote* which is lying in the docks at Port Tewfik."

" Samways, I once knew a Samways," the man gasped. " He was an officer in the Palestine Police, who nearly put me in front of a firing-squad in the days when Vichy France still held Syria."

" Colonel Samways is my father," Jonathan said. " Now do keep quiet while I see what I can do for you."

" There is nothing. I am beyond human aid, my lad," the man replied. " I am dying. Those swine got their knives into my lungs. Is your father still alive ? "

" Yes," Jonathan replied.

" Then tell him that you saw the last moments

of Eric von Thurstein. The Red Cormorant is what they used to call me once upon a time."

It was then Jonathan's turn to gasp. The Red Cormorant had been one of the most dangerous and certainly the most picturesque and romantic of all the German agents in Arab countries. He had been, perhaps, the only man who really deserved to be called the German " Lawrence of Arabia." Even his enemies had been filled with admiration for him, and though they had done everything to capture him, everyone had been secretly glad when news came that Eric von Thurstein had died in battle on Leros Island at the end of the war, fighting to the last ditch for his own country's sake.

" But—but, I thought you were dead years ago," Jonathan replied in bewilderment. " Everyone believes you were killed in action in 1945. How *can* you be the Red Cormorant ? "

" Dying men do not lie, young Samways," von Thurstein said, slowly. " Now listen carefully, for there is much that you can do for me, and there is no time to lose for I have very few minutes left. I have lived mainly because I hoped to be of service should Germany ever lift her bowed and bloody head again, but now I can see little hope of her recovering her honoured place for many years. I have my Hoard. It is mine, my own personal property. It does not belong to the Reich, nor to anyone else, for it is not loot, but my own legal property. In my shoes you will find the paper for which those murdering devils were seeking. Take it. It will lead you to the place where my treasure is hidden."

The dying man paused from sheer weakness, before, summoning all his remaining strength, he resumed.

"Pass me your word of honour that you will not tell the police who I am," he gasped. "I do not want it to be known that the Red Cormorant perished miserably like this, let him be remembered as the naval officer who died facing fearful odds on Leros. Your father is a gallant man and a gentleman, so take my treasure, lad, if you can get it, and use it with my good wishes. Go back to your ship and say nothing about our encounter."

"But I can't do that," Jonathan protested, as, at the fallen man's urgent order, he was removing his shoe from which he took a piece of folded paper sewn in waterproof silk. "I've got to get you to a hospital where they'll see to those wounds of yours."

"Suez Hospital can do nothing for me," the unfortunate man gasped. "No doctor who ever qualified could save my life. I'm sped and I know it, but that does not matter in the least so long as the memory of the Red Cormorant is not tarnished by any rumours of his miserable death in the dust of this filthy town. So promise me that you will leave my corpse where I am now lying and return to your ship without telling anyone that it was I, the Red Cormorant, who died."

" I'll have to tell my father," Jonathan replied.

" That is fit and proper," von Thurstein agreed, his voice very faint and fading fast. " Tell Colonel Samways that the Red Cormorant was relying on his honour when he died. Promise."

" I promise," Jonathan said, slowly. " All the same, I feel that I ought to get help for you."

" There is no need," the voice gasped, and all at once the terrible bubbling of blood in his air-passages grew louder. " *Auf wiedersehen*—— Remember ! "

Very suddenly it was all over. The Red Cormorant had gone to that Valhalla where fighting-men of all races, creeds and colours are welcomed when their last blow is struck and their course is run. Jonathan staggered to his feet ; all his instincts were to run and summon the police, but the memory of his word of honour halted him. The sobering thought also rose that, with blood on his clothes, a wound in his side, and a stabbed man at his feet, he would need to do a lot of explaining if the police did find him. There is little consideration for a European who is found in suspicious circumstances in Egypt nowadays. At the very best he might be detained in custody for weeks while leisurely investigations were being made; at the worst he might stand trial for murder. Then, too, there was this precious paper which the Red Cormorant had entrusted to him, which, if it was as valuable as the dead man had declared it to be, would also need a lot of explanation if it was discovered on his person by already suspicious police.

He all but panicked as he remembered that if he did not hurry, there would be an explanation due to Mr. Chalmers as soon as he returned to his ship. If that happened it would be very difficult to keep his word to poor, dead Eric von Thurstein. As there was nothing he could do for the unfortunate German, he decided he had better get away as quickly as he could.

He was only just in time in making his exit, for he was scarcely gone before three shadowy figures slunk down the sordid alley and started to ransack the clothes of the limp corpse lying in the dust. The leading robber cursed softly when nothing except a few piastres were found, for they were looking for papers.

" I thought I saw someone pass out of the end of the lane and turn towards Port Tewfik as we came up, O Abdul Rahman Bey," one of the kneeling figures whispered.

" Mention no names, you fool," the third man hissed. " If you wish to keep your tongue safe in your mouth learn to stop it babbling names. Be dumb, idiot! "

The men, however, persisted that he had seen someone leaving the lane and the leader sprang to his feet.

“ Then we must seize him. Maybe it was some dog who knew the true identity of this carrion and, like a jackal sneaked in to steal the prey of the eagles who had killed their quarry. Come, let us go after this mysterious stranger, but let us also be careful on the causeway for fear that we meet a police patrol. Our faces are too well known to those sneaking catchpolls ; if they recognise us and so learn that we have come in from the bare hills of Sinai, all Egypt will be turned out to lay us by the heels.”

The three figures flitted like shadows down the lane, but by the time they emerged Jonathan was halfway down the causeway and hurrying to get back to the docks in time to satisfy the Chief Officer. His white uniform betrayed him, for the keen-eyed Arabs saw the glimmer of it as the lad passed under one of the street-lamps. Running fast with a loping, wolf-like tread, they flitted so swiftly over the tumbled boulders and piled earth flanking the railway which lies between the two roads and forms the central part of the causeway that, by the time they were a few yards short of the Port Tewfik end they were abreast of Jonathan, although still on the other road. The leader snarled a brief command, and was instantly obeyed by his companions who with one accord turned left and darted across the railway towards the sailor on the further side.

Jonathan was so distressed and harassed by all that had occurred since he left the house of kindly Mustafa Effendi, that he had not the least inkling of danger until he suddenly saw the three figures racing towards him in the dimmer area half-way between two of the widely-spaced lamps, and noted with terror that they wore the dress of Bedouins from the desert, a strange garb for night-prowlers in the sea-port of Suez ! Instinctively he never had the least doubt of their intentions, from the moment he first saw them he knew that this was a murderous attack directed at himself, and connected with that murdered man whom he had attended. Jonathan's nerve almost cracked in those terrible split-seconds while the dagger-men were charging towards him ; he was completely unarmed, he did not have even so much as a walking-stick with which to fight for his life, while he could see steel glimmering in the murderous hands of the sinister trio.

They were skilled, too, in their deadly trade, and were working out clever tactics, for while the central man dashed straight at Jonathan, those on his flanks were fanning out to cut off any chance of his retreat towards Suez or dashing onwards towards Port Tewfik. Three hundred yards ahead he saw the blazing lights at the dock-gates, which spelled safety, while, a short way beyond them were the electric lamp-clusters of his own ship, and the clatter of hammers and riveting-machines where the workmen toiled through the night.

He took all this in in a flash, and thanking his lucky stars that his upbringing had been so different from the normal one a British boy receives at home, he paused while his mind worked at lightning speed. Jonathan was a big fellow, only half an inch short of six foot, and was broad with it, but he knew that if he allowed them to get near enough to use their blades he would not stand a chance against the three hardy Bedouin warriors. Neither could he hope to dodge them on that narrow causeway and, long before any help could reach him, they would have sunk their knives into his body, robbed him and got safely away into the slums of Suez.

He was really up against it. He was facing death. His experience of this bloodstained Middle East allowed him no illusions about what his fate was likely to be unless he did something in the next few seconds to save himself. This was no casual attack by footpads; they would never have waited until he was so close to the bright lights of the dock-gates and the armed police who stood guard there. He had been deliberately pursued from the scene of the killing of the Red Cormorant; the Bedouin were probably the German's murderers, madly anxious to recover the oil-silk wrapped package they knew he must be carrying. Death was very near ; these brutes, already guilty of one murder that night, would not have the least hesitation in slaying him as well. It would be useless to halt, in the hope of saving his life, surrender his few possessions and submit to whatever brutality they might inflict, for they must slay him to cover their own retreat along the narrow causeway.

The man in the centre was not twenty feet away, but there was still the fence hedging the railway between them, but it was a flimsy barrier which could not delay a determined attacker for more than a few seconds. The Arab ahead was already over it and was crouched in the roadway, knife-blade aglitter, ready to deal with him, waiting only to see in which direction the victim might try to run. Behind, the third assassin was cursing softly as he also climbed over the wire and felt one of its barbs scratch his thigh.

CHAPTER 2

CHENG LOO WATCHES

ONLY the sea remained open to Jonathan. On that side alone there was no enemy, and he cast a swift glance at the water, bespangled with the long lanes of glittering light from the causeway's lamps as the centre man of the attacking-party climbed over the top of the six-foot fence. Then came inspiration in the recollection that inland Bedouin, men from the desert tribes, seldom know how to swim. He could not hope to avoid them on the solid causeway, but if he entered the water Jonathan's own skill might cancel the odds against him.

Without a second thought he whipped round and turned his back on his snarling assailants and before they realised what he meant to do he had climbed to the crest of the low pile of boulders facing westerly, and with a long, shallow dive was hurtling through the waters of Suez Bay. Then, as his feet left the land the thought of sharks crashed through his mind—he swiftly fought down his terror and took comfort in the thought that the sea-tigers were not nearly so imminent a peril as those land-sharks of Bedouin whom he had left behind. As he surfaced he heard them chattering and cursing as angrily as enraged monkeys. Something hissed past his ears and splashed with a flicker of steel within three inches of his left cheek. One of the Bedouins had thrown his dagger at the swimming head, and was so expert a marksman that he had missed his target only by the narrowest of margins.

Jonathan was so much afraid that his nerve became steely; he had never been so close to a violent death in all his days so that all his instincts came automatically to his aid. Cold terror, an incredible loathing, and a fierce determination possessed his mind as he struck away from the causeway with the swiftest "crawl" stroke he had ever used in his life. Even the thought of the lurking sharks was obliterated, temporarily, from his mind by the need to get away from those murderous Arabs gibbering their rage from the roadway. Very soon he was outside their limit of vision, but it was not until he was a couple of hundred yards offshore and slowly grew certain that they could not swim, that he paused to consider what he should do next.

The first thing was to decide what his enemies' reactions might be. Obviously they would expect him to swim towards the bright lights of the dock-gates and would, in consequence, hide themselves somewhere near where they anticipated his landing. As he staggered out of the water they could slip a dagger into him before he could defend himself, for the Bedouin are as skilled in ambushes as were the Redskins of America a hundred years ago. Before he realised his enemies had seen him wading in he would be dead, without the least outcry aroused to alarm the policemen standing on guard a few hundred feet away.

Jonathan's early experiences of Bedouin tribes had taught him to respect their cunning and their audacity so that he was not in the least danger of underestimating them, as a young man, fresh from home might have done. He made up his mind to swim home the long way round, to pass the end of the docks and thus come alongside the *Symondsbury Mote* from seawards, where he would be invisible to anyone on the wharf. His flesh fairly crawled at the thought of the grey, obscene forms of the scores of sharks which he had seen in the turgid waters of the docks as they policed the sides of the ships, waiting to snap up any edible rubbish that the cooks and crews might dump overboard. The sea-tigers must be risked, however. Bad as they were they seemed a lesser danger than those three warriors lurking in the shadows of the causeway.

But though they might indeed be the lesser of the two evils they were still most terribly present to his imagination and Jonathan got only the coldest comfort from comparing his dangers during those twenty minutes that he was swimming through the warm waters of Suez Harbour. Even the fact that he did not so much as meet a single shark did not cheer him in the least, for there was not a second when he was not almost certain that he already felt the swirl of a great, steel-hard, torpedo-shaped body turning over to seize him. The anticipation of a painful and terrible end in a sea-monster's belly was almost as bad as the realisation, as Jonathan has often since admitted.

His greatest self-control was needed not to shout for help so as to bring the police or a longshoreman rowing out to rescue him. Only his logical reasoning that it would do no good prevented his doing so. By the time they answered his shrieks and launched a boat he would have been as long in the water as if he had carried quietly on towards *Symondsbury Mote.* Then too, there was the startling fact that his assailants were not the usual city-thieves but Bedouin, which meant that they must have been in pursuit of the man they had murdered, and that the crime was not due to a sudden affray. They would therefore be keen to get hold of the man who had seized the package which they had risked so much to get. It would be little use to save his life for the moment, only to be trailed down and stabbed by the desert daggermen when they discovered his identity later. If they had the least idea who he was Jonathan knew that his doom would be sealed, so he made up his mind to risk the sea-tigers and to make his own way back to the ship in the hope that no secret watcher on shore would see to which of the many vessels he went.

The first time he saw a shark was when he actually touched the steel sides of *Symondsbury Mote*, at the very moment he laid hold of the Jacob's ladder left for the use of the stevedore-shift which came across from the landing by boat. A swirl in the rubbish-covered water stirred the oil-scum in wavelets and set the cabbage-stalks and potato-peelings scurrying so that Jonathan had to fight down a scream as he felt the faintest brush from something that felt like very coarse sand-paper against his feet. A shark was investigating this new titbit which had so suddenly come within its ken! If it had not been already well-fed it would certainly have struck home, but as its belly was full it showed scarcely more than a gentle interest in this fresh arrival.

Jonathan fought down his panic, although it cost him a terrific effort to do so. Probably the only thing which allowed him to do so was the certainty that if he was detected coming inboard the Mate would make such a fuss that the Egyptian *ghaffirs*, the paid watchmen at the head of the accommodation-ladder, would hear about it, and when they went ashore, at the end of their tour of duty, they would gossip. Thus the Bedouins would learn that a young officer had swum off to his ship and so the secret of his identity would be known and all his precautions be made useless. Jonathan was relying on the attackers believing that he was merely the normal, ordinary sailorman who has little idea of what happens ashore in countries like theirs, and consequently that he would easily betray himself. They could have no idea that their quarry had been brought up among Arabs and their ways of doing things.

Jonathan climbed the Jacob's ladder to the point whence he could see over the top of her tall sides ; his eyes were level with the upper deck planking as he peered over the scuppers. All was quiet, no one appeared to be moving about, while the height of the midship superstructure rose like a wall to his left with its ladder less than a dozen feet away. If only he could reach the saloon-deck on the top of that superstructure he would stand an excellent chance of gaining his cabin without being seen. He mentally blessed the chance that as he was the senior cadet he had a cabin to himself, the other two apprentices sharing another on the other side of the vessel. If he could reach his bunk and turn in without being seen, he should be safe.

The lad raised himself, rapidly, and slid inboard over the rail, lying prone along it to avoid rising too high, and then, flitting across the deck, he reached the ladder and started to ascend it, when he heard the murmur of voices only a few feet away. Halting sharply in his tracks he recognised the voice of the Chief Officer. If Mr. Chalmers saw him in his bedraggled, drenched, oil-stained and blood-fouled condition there would be only too much publicity, and, when the murder became known the chances were that he, Jonathan, would be detained for questioning after the ship had sailed. He had no illusions as to what his fate would be if he was kept in Egypt, for those three murderous slinkers-in-the-shadows knew he possessed the paper which they had missed from the Red Cormorant's corpse, and they were not likely to leave anything untried in their efforts to regain it.

Very, very gently, Jonathan descended the five or six steps he had mounted, and as he did so heard the Chief Officer say, lazily, that he must be getting along to the "half-deck," which is the old windjammer term for the apprentices' quarters, to make sure that the lads were safely tucked up. The Chief Engineer, who was sitting in the deck-chair beside him, replied that he need not worry for a few more minutes and so they resumed their discussion, which, so far as Jonathan could make out, was a long argument about the number of days that a Chinaman had survived on a raft without food and water, after his ship was sunk by a raider in the South Atlantic.

There was another route, for by going along the alleyway on the main-deck Jonathan could reach the midship stairs leading from the passengers' dining-room to the saloon-deck, but there was grave risk that on this public thoroughfare he might meet some of them returning from a party at the French Club in Port Tewfik. The French Club is the best European meeting place in that part of the world, the Canal Staff and their families are usually glad to extend its hospitality to Europeans detained in their sweltering port. That was a risk that he was forced to take, however, for there was not the least hope of getting past the two reclining officers at the head of the ladder.

Boldness paid, as it usually does, and Jonathan reached his cabin without, so far as he knew, being seen by anyone. He was not aware, however, that a Chinese cabin-steward had seen his bedraggled figure slinking along the alleyway. Cheng Loo was not the man to broadcast things he saw, for years of intrigue in his own land had been followed by exile and his taking up domestic service afloat. He saw much, and said extremely little. He crouched into an empty cabin as the senior cadet passed him, so, scarcely daring to believe his own good luck, Jonathan stood in his cabin, quite sure that he had reached it in complete secrecy, peeling off his foul clothing.

He turned the little silk-wrapped package which he had been given by the dying man, over and over in his hand, and then placed it aside on a small shelf while he washed his face and filthy body. He had removed the worst of the muck when he was electrified to hear the Chief Officer speaking to the steward.

"'Did you do this?' Jonathan demanded turning on the Chinese steward."

“ Yes, Mister Chalmers, sir,” the sing-song voice of Cheng Loo replied. “ Mr. Samways is in cabin.”

Wondering how the yellow-skinned, pock-marked villain could possibly know that fact, Jonathan dived between the sheets and picked up a book in the few seconds before the Chief Officer knocked on the door and came in.

“ I didn’t see you coming aboard, Samways,” he boomed. “ Better get your light out ; I need you good and early in the morning. The Captain is going ashore to pay a call on the Egyptian Governor and he wants you to accompany him as his interpreter. Nice soft job for you, my lad ; I had meant to give you a bit of chipping to do. No time to learn like this ; it’ll teach you how to do it when you get your own ticket. Which, by the way, I doubt if you’ll ever get, if you lie awake in your bunk to all hours reading adventure stories. What is that book ? ” and he stretched out his hand for the volume the lad was holding.

“ It’s a sea-yarn I used to like when I was a kid in Palestine, sir,” Jonathan replied, and showed him a battered copy of “ Sea Urchin’s Second Charter.” He looked up. “ You see, sir, I knew the author, Douglas Stanhope. He was an officer in the Palestine Police in the old days. He was my father’s second-in-command at Nazareth for a couple of years.”

“ Pah ! ” the weather-beaten old officer snorted.

“ It would suit you better to read the ‘ Principles of Seamanship,’ or else be learning about manifests and cargo-stowage, instead of filling your apology for a mind with that balderdash. Adventures like that don’t happen nowadays. Going to sea is just as tame as bus-driving. More so, for we don’t have fool pedestrians to bother about. Good-night. Don’t forget, your freshest set of whites, clean buttons and a shave ! You’re to pay a state call in attendance on the Captain remember. Adventures ! Bah ! ”

With a disgusted “ Good-night, Samways,” Mr. Chalmers departed, while Jonathan secretly and, to his almost hysterical amusement, wondered what the old man would say if he had the least idea of the adventures that his young subordinate had experienced that very night ! It was just as well that he had no such inkling and Jonathan, after slipping the bolt on his door, quickly disposed of his stained white uniform, which was past all laundering or repair, by wrapping it around a big steel marline-spike and dropping it through the wide porthole into the water. Then he noticed the long scratch which the dagger-point had made in his skin, coated it with iodine, and, as the bleeding had long since stopped, paid it no further attention. After that it was easy to slip along to the bathroom at the end of the alleyway and make himself clean. He saw Cheng Loo as he returned and as the impassive-faced

Chinaman stepped back to let him pass, the lad looked at him and thanked him for telling the Mate that he was in his cabin.

" You saved my bacon, Cheng Loo," Jonathan grinned. " By the way you can have that pair of maroon socks from my middle drawer if you still want them. They're quite new; I've never worn them and I know you covet the things. By the way, how did you happen to know I was in my cabin?"

" Cheng Loo is cabin-steward, Mr. Samways," he replied. " In Suez are plenty thieves and Cheng Loo is good steward. Cheng Loo sees everything. Cheng Loo is very grateful for munificent present of socks and thanks you. Can he bring his unworthy self to your cabin and get socks now?"

Jonathan laughed and made a chaffing remark while he led the way back to his room. It was not until the Chinese steward had gone, as impassive as ever with his prized socks, that he realised the man must have seen the strange little silk-wrapped package, all foul and glistening with oil and bearing the dark stains of blood, lying on the shelf screwed to the after bulkhead of the white-enamelled cabin. But the lad's misgivings were quickly allayed—there could be no danger from Cheng Loo, who had just proved such a friend in need when he could so easily have given him away. He dismissed the incident from his mind in the excitement of opening the package, which seemed to be so important that men were prepared to do murder to get hold of it.

Jonathan bolted his door before he slit the silk and then, holding the fouled covering in his hands, dried it carefully and laid it aside in a manilla envelope. Its contents, four small sheets of thin, tough India paper, were quite dry and, to his surprise, were covered by thin, regular lines of the most precise meticulous Arabic lettering. Jonathan promptly turned to what would have been the back page of an ordinary Western letter, and starting at the top right-hand corner, began to read " backwards."

His first puzzled reaction was that the whole thing was gibberish ! The Arabic characters and letters were perfect enough, the six main accent-symbols were clearly drawn as well, while there were also excellent figures, but the language meant nothing ! Puzzled, yet knowing that it must be important, he began to read it out phonetic-ally, to pronounce the words aloud and, as he did so, a great light broke on him ; the writing was in Arabic lettering but the language was some sort of German. A German had written it in Arabic not in the usual Western script, using the quanti-ties of the letter-sounds to express his own tongue.

" That foxes me for the time being," he muttered in deep exasperation. " I wonder what language it is—it's very like German, but it's not that. I'm not able to make a proper translation and as it's so important I'd be a fool to show it to anyone else. I'll hide it until I can show it to Dad and let him attend to it. The only question is where in the world shall I put it ? "

He studied his little cabin and knew that there was no possible hiding-place where a determined searcher would not discover it. There was nowhere on the ship for that matter. If this document was so terribly vital, as the murder of poor von Thurstein seemed to prove it to be, then it must be extremely valuable and that meant there would be determined attempts to find it. For the first time the bland pock-marked face of Cheng Loo grew sinister—if enquiries were made by people ashore, the Chinaman could tell them about the package whose wrappings he had seen.

The only safe place was in the Mail ! Jonathan quickly pulled out an envelope, folded the four sheets, put in a small note, addressed it to his father, and, placing a stamp on it, opened his door and looked out. Cheng Loo was nowhere to be seen—the corridor looked empty, but Jonathan feared that the slit-eyed Cantonese would be watching from some hidden lair. Hiding the letter inside his bath-robe's breast, Jonathan stepped out, and, sure enough, met the Chinaman in the foyer outside his block of cabins.

" Too hot for sleep, Cheng Loo," Jonathan

murmured. " I'm going out on deck to get a breath of fresh air."

" Yes, very hot," the man agreed. " Be much more better when honourable engineer officer repair air-conditioning mechanism. Was switched off to-night at eight-bells, not to come on again until morning so Third Engineer tell honourable Chief Steward."

" So that's what's wrong is it," Jonathan remarked. " Anyway, I'll snatch a breath of the night's coolness," and with that he went on deck. He waited only long enough to make sure the Chinese steward was not following him, and then slipped down to the corridor outside the Purser's Office, where, after a glance in both directions, he posted the letter to his father in the passenger's mail-box.

When he had done so he went up on deck for a few minutes, but feeling utterly weary and with the reaction of all that he had been through oppressing him he returned quietly to his cabin. He did not see Cheng Loo on his way, and so was rather surprised to see him come out of his, Jonathan's, own cabin. A broad smile lit the yellow face.

" I try to make you more comfortable, Mr. Samways, sir," the steward beamed. " You give me nice gift of maroon socks, I tidy your room. I bring fan from Brazilian merchant's stateroom so that you keep cool while air-conditioning system not operative."

" Thank you, Cheng Loo," Jonathan replied gratefully, all his suspicions of the man evaporating in face of this kindly act. " That was really good of you."

He was far too tired to sit up reading, and with the cool draught of the electric-fan swinging back and forth across the cabin was soon asleep.

It was not until he was shaving in the early morning and looking over the crisp white uniform which Cheng Loo had laid out for him that he remembered the soiled wrappings of the package the Red Cormorant had given him. It was far too dangerous a thing to leave lying about and he felt like kicking himself for his carelessness. He must get rid of it. That would be easy enough when he went on deck, and so, bending down, he looked for the envelope in which he had placed it.

It was gone! And, although he searched every square inch of his cabin, he found not the least trace of it. Someone had taken it away during the night! Jonathan felt an icy trickle of sweat run down his spine at the thought that someone now knew that the Red Cormorant's package was in his possession; it was he who had gone off with it after the death of the famous Secret Agent.

" You looking for something, Mr. Samways, sir?" the bland voice of Cheng Loo enquired. Jonathan wheeled, for he had not heard the door opening. The brown, slit-like, oblique eyes studied him quite dispassionately, there was not the slightest hint of concern in their twinkling depths. " Much better you hurry, sir ; honourable Captain's breakfast already served. If you not quick you will feel pangs of hunger very soon, for honourable Captain not wait for cadet to eat."

Jonathan trembled on the verge of accusing the steward of stealing the silk wrapping. Only his trained caution saved him. What use would it be to mention the matter to Cheng Loo ; if the fellow was in the pay of the murderers he would deny it. If he was innocent he had only to say that he had thought it was rubbish and thrown it away with the other refuse. There was nothing Jonathan could do about it. Cheng Loo could not be questioned, and so, with a last look into the man's slant eyes, Jonathan gulped and turned away.

" Honourable Mr. Samways not too well this morning ? " Cheng Loo queried. " If feeling indisposed I will ask honourable doctor for tonic. No ? "

" No ! " Jonathan snapped, and strode away to the saloon for his breakfast, doubt and terror his companions. Cheng Loo was a mystery and Jonathan thought of the yarns he had heard about the man having been a prominent official in Nationalist China. The other stewards of his own race in the ship certainly treated him with a deferential fear that was so obvious that even the white officers had often commented on the strange fact.

CHAPTER 3

FEAR ON THE SUEZ CANAL

JONATHAN returned aboard with the Captain about half-an-hour before noon, and though he had kept his ears and eyes wide open during the Governor's reception, and also while they were waiting among the officers and secretaries in the ante-room, he had not heard a single word about any murder in the back-streets of Suez during the previous night.

That was scarcely surprising for if a dozen humble longshoremen or slum-dwellers had been slain, it was not likely that a foreign ship-captain would hear the matter being discussed in the Governor's *serai*, his office-residence. It was even more unlikely that the assassination of a man who had once enjoyed world-wide fame would be being talked over so soon after its occurrence. In fact the lad had heard no mention of the street-killing during the days while *Symondsbury Mote's* repairs were being finished and she turned, north-bound, up the Canal on her way to Port Said at its Mediterranean end.

He had kept a quiet watch on Cheng Loo but that worthy had not even gone ashore so far as

Jonathan could tell. He had remained faithfully guarding his block of passenger-cabins and diligently shooing away any Egyptians who came too close. After a while Jonathan began to lose his distrust of the pock-marked Chinaman and to believe that he was nothing but the cheerful, honest, loyal and not too intelligent soul that he appeared to be. It was not until an hour before they were due to leave the dockside at Port Tewfik that he began to doubt this estimate of the Cantonese steward.

It happened while Jonathan was hurrying to the bridge, his leaving-harbour station as senior cadet. The other two cadets were placed one with Mr. Chalmers on the forecastle, the junior on the poop with the Second Officer, but Jonathan's job was to keep the rough-log which recorded the timings of the several evolutions and engine-movements so that they could be entered accurately into the Fair Log for the owners in London. He was starting to climb the ladder to the boat-deck when he saw Cheng Loo talking to an Egyptian dressed in the uniform of one of the new Assistant Pilots which the new regime has placed in the Canal service, but as Jonathan could think of no excuse for stopping he continued his journey to the bridge.

He was kept very busy there until the ship had entered the Canal and was running northwards, but he was surprised when the traffic-signal at

El Kubri Station, the first of the control-points north of Suez, was suddenly raised against them as they drew nearer and *Symondsbury Mote* was compelled to moor to the huge bollards which stud the banks throughout the Canal's whole length. A party of officials came aboard at El Kubri, and he saw they had a few uniformed policemen with them, but nothing much happened before the ship started again and headed once more towards the southern end of the Great Bitter Lake.

Geneifa Canal Station was in sight when the officer of the watch beckoned Jonathan over to him and told him that he was wanted in the captain's cabin. He was, naturally, very surprised, but descended the bridge-ladder to the deck beneath where, knocking on the door near the bottom, he was gruffly bidden to enter. He stepped inside the cabin and found Captain Brooks, a very worried frown on his red, weather-beaten face, sitting at his desk, facing a smooth-faced, olive-skinned man who wore a scarlet tarboush on his oily, black hair, and was lounging insolently on the broadside settee. They both looked up as the cadet entered.

"Well, Bimbashi," Captain Brooks said, in a grating, hostile voice, giving the man in plain clothes his military title. "This is Samways, my senior cadet. Perhaps you will say whatever it is you want to tell him here, and in my presence."

"I would prefer to question him in my own office in Fayed, Captain Brooks," the officer replied. "I demand that he should be placed ashore and submit to my interrogation."

Jonathan gasped, his eyes goggling in astonishment, wondering what all this might mean. A battle-royal, silent but very intense and bitter, was, he could sense, raging between the Old Man and this sleek-looking Egyptian in the fez, who was so evidently a police officer.

"Have you a warrant for Samways' arrest?" the Captain demanded, "and if you have, on what charge do you wish to hold him?"

The *bimbashi* spread his hands in a deprecating fashion and raised his palms to shoulder-level. He gave a shrug and smiled apologetically.

"No, no, Captain," he protested. "There is no question of arrests or of warrants. We merely wish to ask this young gentleman a few questions, and we think that they can be answered more easily in our offices. That is all."

"Then Samways will miss his passage home," the Old Man retorted angrily. "We're not staying at Port Said, you know. I'm bound straight through. If I do allow this young man to go he will never reach Port Said in time to join us after you have had your little fun-and-games with him. No, without a proper warrant, I absolutely refuse to hand him over, and, even if you produce a warrant, I will not surrender him before I have seen the British Consul in Port Said. You may put him under arrest if you care to formulate a definite charge, and I will allow you to hold him under guard in his cabin until we have seen the Consul. But I will not allow him to be taken ashore at Geneifa as you request. In any case what have you got against him ? "

" That, I am afraid is something which I am not allowed to disclose," the man replied, his face still suave and his manner apologetic. " All I have been told myself is that I am to take him ashore and bring him to the Governor's office in Ismailia as quickly as I can. I warn you, Captain," he went on, threateningly, " you will find it dangerous to refuse."

" You can't expect me to allow one of my junior officers to be taken off my ship in such a summary fashion as this," Captain Brooks roared, and, jumping upright he thumped the table. " You make no charge, you have no warrant of arrest, and yet you expect me to tamely give up a British subject who is a member of my crew. No, Bimbashi, I absolutely refuse."

" May I remind you that Mr. Samways is not a British subject," the man broke in, a polite smile on his face. " He was born in Palestine—in Jerusalem Old City to be exact, a place which is now outside the borders of the present State of Israel. He is, I suppose, a subject of the King of Jordania. I fancy that the ruler of his native land will not object to the government of Egypt, their ally, being allowed to detain him."

Jonathan's blood ran cold. Of course it was all nonsense that he was not a British subject, although he certainly had been born in the walled city of Old Jerusalem in the days when his father was District Superintendent of Police there, but that did not detract from his British status. With a sudden sinking feeling he saw that this point was troubling Captain Brooks, who did not want his ship to be delayed by technicalities which might keep her tied to Port Said anchorage for weeks. The Red Diamond Line would be none too pleased with one of their Masters who cost them most of their profits by allowing such a piling-up of costs and crew wages.

'Is this true, Samways ?" he barked. "Were you born in Jerusalem ?"

Jonathan felt real fear. If he admitted it nothing was surer than that the Old Man would allow this senior officer to remove him. In the changed aspect of international matters, it might have been dangerous for him to refuse to give up even a British subject if there was a criminal charge against him.

"My passport is in my cabin, sir," Jonathan replied. "It is British and was granted only two years ago, so there can be no question as to whether I am a British subject or not. Please, sir," he went on, addressing himself directly to the Captain, " may I be told what this is all about? What am I supposed to have done that the Egyptian Police should want to arrest me?"

" Ask this gentleman," Captain Brooks snorted, and the accentuation that he placed on the last word was neither respectful nor friendly. The *bimbashi*, however, seeing that his trick had failed, was still as smilingly urbane as ever.

" I assure you, Mr. Samways, that we have no suspicions of you," he said, quietly. " We wish only to make some routine inquiries and believe that they can be done better in one of our offices where we have all our dossiers and equipment readily available, than here in a ship. But, as your captain will not agree to your temporary absence, I am afraid that I must go ashore at Geneifa to make contact with my authorities who will, doubtlessly, give me further instructions, which I will execute before you get to Port Said. May I suggest that you have a bag packed and be ready to leave the ship by the time you reach Lake Timsah, or, at the very latest, before the vessel passes El Kantara."

El Kantara is halfway between Ismailia, the middle of the canal and Port Said, and is the place where the railway from Palestine crosses the canal on its way to Cairo.

" With your permission, Captain," the *bimbashi* went on, " I will now proceed ashore. You will forgive me if I mention that I feel bound to report your non-co-operation with the State Police to my authorities. I am afraid that the British Ambassador will not be too pleased when he hears about it from my Minister of the Interior."

That remark shook the Captain. A seaman to his finger-tips he detested and disliked politicians and, because he knew nothing about them, was very much afraid of the bad effects they might exercise on his career.

" If you like to go voluntarily, Samways," he said, looking rather hopefully at his senior cadet, " I shall be only too pleased to give you leave to go ashore."

" I'll bet you will," Jonathan thought to himself, although he was very careful not to let his thoughts show on his face. Aloud, he said, " I don't understand, sir. I can't begin to think why I am wanted by the Egyptian Police. If this gentleman will only tell me why they wish to question me I'll be only too glad to help them. But I won't go off this ship, unless I'm thrown off, and if I am, my father will want to know the reason why. You'll remember, sir, that he is Member of Parliament for the division of West Pyemore, and so may cause quite a stir when he hears about it."

Captain Brooks, driven to desperation between these two threats of political interference, bellowed like a mad bull. He had quite forgotten that Colonel Samways was an M.P. Between British

Ambassadors, Egyptian Ministers of the Interior and English M.P.'s he had reached his limit, and thereupon detonated in sheer exasperation. He turned on the still smiling *bimbashi*, and snapped that he would be willing to deal with him only when he came aboard armed with legal warrant, meanwhile would he mind making his ship a little sweeter by taking his malodorous carcase ashore?

Jonathan, still terribly anxious, went back to the bridge to his own station, to meet the curious looks of the French Canal-pilot and the officers on duty. He could not imagine why the *bimbashi* should have come for him at all, let alone have behaved in so unusual a manner. The lad was very scared that he might be dragged ashore further north in the Canal and so it was with anxiety that he watched the *bimbashi*, and two uniformed policemen being landed on the pier at Geneifa Station, before the *Symondsbury Mote* turned her shapely bows into the channel dredged through the shallows of the Great Bitter Lake.

He was quite sure of course that it all tied in somewhere with the murder of the Red Cormorant and the loss of the package he had been carrying, that mysterious document which, by then, must already be at his father's house in Dorset, as it had been despatched by Air Mail three days earlier. What did they hope to learn from him, and how did they know that he had been present when the German died? To that there could be only one answer—Cheng Loo! He was the only man who had seen Jonathan come aboard that night, and it was almost certain that it was he who had taken the fouled silken wrappings in which the papers had been sewn. Cheng Loo, then, must either be one of the same gang who had slaughtered the Red Cormorant, or else he had come into their employ since the murder.

Jonathan was in a growing state of nerve-strain as the tall monument commemorating the attack by the Turks on the Suez Canal in the First World War was passed just south of Lake Timsah, and when, at Ismailia, a police speed-boat put three senior officers in uniform aboard *Symondsbury Mote*, he was frankly terrified, and asked permission to descend to his cabin, hoping to pack things he might need during his sojourn in an Egyptian jail.

He opened his door and almost sprang backwards against the opposite bulkhead in the alleyway as Cheng Loo appeared at the door of the cabin. For one fleeting instant the yellow mask of a face showed anxiety and then, as though a rubber had erased every feeling from it, the Chinaman looked up.

"I was cleaning out your cabin, Mr. Samways," he said smoothly. "I beg to report that some unworthy and unprincipled person has ransacked it, casting all your clothes and other treasured possessions in a muddle on the floor and on to your honourable bed. Please to come in and see how I have nearly finished putting straight unexampled confusion, and also to check your possessions, so that you may know if anything has been stolen."

It was true enough as Jonathan saw at once. The drawers had been pulled roughly out of their slides, and searched by being upturned on the carpet. His shelf of books lay all which-ways, while a knife had obviously been used to inspect his mattress and pillows, a mass of feathers from the latter making an imitation snow-drift in one corner. Even the plumbing of his folding wash-basin had been torn about. Someone had made a most ruthless and complete search of the young cadet's cabin.

"Did you do this?" Jonathan demanded, turning on the Chinese steward, his fist clenched, his eyes flashing in rage. All his own fear and resentment, all his terrors of the Egyptian police mounted in one wave to make him fighting-mad. Cheng Loo did not so much as bat an eyelid, nor flinch in the least degree.

"If the humble son of my father wished to search your room, honourable Mr. Samways," he said, quietly, "he would not conduct investigations in this crude manner. He knows all possible hiding-places in your cabin so that he would experience no need to make mess such as this."

That was very true and Jonathan's fist loosened while the red flush on his face receded. The clever yellow devil might have rigged all this confusion to make it look as though it had been wrecked by some outsider, and at the thought the English lad's anger rose again. But before he had a chance to speak, Williams, the junior cadet, came running along the corridor.

"The Old Man's howling for you, Jonathan," he announced. "You're to lay along to his cabin at once and he's got the darned place packed tight with policemen. Golly, what *have* you been doing? There's another couple of dozen Gippie coppers standing by in an armed launch. Looks to me by the way they're taking precautions as though they think you're Dick Turpin and Billy the Kid all knocked into one."

Jonathan had not even the urge to snarl at the youngster; sick at heart and completely mystified by all that had happened to him during the last few days, he told Cheng Loo to pack a small bag for him, and then, with lagging footsteps, turned and followed Williams towards the Captain's cabin.

Just as had happened further south, the Captain had a police-officer sitting opposite to him, with two more at his elbows. For a moment Jonathan scarcely looked at them, his attention was focused on the Captain who stared back gloomily at him.

"This is young Samways," Captain Brooks said. "Will you tell him or shall I?"

" You are his captain, sir, I suggest that you should have the telling." The burly senior officer in the khaki uniform and gleaming Sam Browne belt looked up, and as he did so, Jonathan shouted in excitement, and started to move towards him.

CHAPTER 4

PERIL ALL THE WAY

"ALI BEY!" Jonathan called out in sheer gladness, overjoyed at finding a friend at the very moment when everything had seemed so dark and hostile. "I am awfully glad to see you, and I know that Dad will be thrilled to hear that I've seen you."

The Egyptian *miralai*, which is a rank equivalent to a colonel in the British service, was already on his feet to welcome the youngster.

"It is my old friend Jonathan!" he said, joyously. "Little Jonathan whom I watched growing from childhood and is now a fine young man." He held the tall lad well away from him, his swarthy face alight with friendship. "And what a man you've grown into, Jonathan Samways." His eyes roved admiringly over the bulk of the young cadet. "I was a fool not to recognise your name in the signal that your captain sent us by radio."

Ali Bey Fayoumi, *miralai* in the Frontier Districts Administration, had served his apprenticeship as an officer of armed Constabulary in that grand school of the Palestine Police where, for many years, he had worked under Colonel Samways, and, as was nearly always the case, there had been a very close link between British and local officers. He was laughing now, as he kept his hands on Jonathan's shoulders.

"You need not worry any more, Captain Brooks," the *miralai* said, "Even if we wanted Jonathan for some awful crime I am sure we should find some way to save him. No," and his face grew serious, "those were not members of any of our Egyptian police-forces who boarded you down south. We have been frankly puzzled why they should have taken the risk of trying to kidnap a member of a British cargo-liner's crew. Can *you* tell us, Jonathan," and the kindly, hazel eyes looked shrewdly into the lad's grey ones.

"I'm afraid not, Ali Bey," Jonathan replied, for he could not see that the death of the Red Cormorant could have anything to do with him. He was afraid, also, that if he made any mention of it, he would be detained in Eygpt and that was a fate he dreaded above everything else. If he was kept back nothing seemed surer than that this mysterious and sinister organisation which had already tried so hard to capture him, would get him in its clutches. Consequently, he said nothing, even offering the bright suggestion that the would-be kidnappers might be people who nursed some grudge against his father for something that had happened long ago.

Ali Bey shook his grizzled head in deep thought. "I do not think that that is likely," he said, slowly. "However, they may have been impudent enough to try to snatch the son of a member of the British Parliament, hoping to hold him to ransom. Come to think of it, that is not too unlikely. We have some very bad political underground organisations which are definitely criminal in their ways of doing things. If they had succeeded in kidnapping Jonathan from a British ship it might suit the perverted purposes of some of them, for the resulting diplomatic trouble, in which London would accuse our people of not being able to maintain security on an international waterway like the Canal, might easily cause the fall of our Government, and so give these extremists a chance to do what they wish."

A silence fell over the men in the cabin. Jonathan kept very quiet; he knew how wrong was their theory but it would be most convenient, and save a whole lot of trouble, if these officers accepted Ali Bey's suggestion. Jonathan was so frightened of what might happen to him if he was taken ashore that he was determined to keep very quiet, and in any case, he could not tell them the facts without betraying his word of honour to that poor, dying German, who had once been almost as romantic a figure as was Lawrence of Arabia himself.

"Thank you, Ali Bey," Captain Brooks said

quietly. " I cannot tell you how glad I am to learn that I shall not have any trouble when we reach Port Said. Now, as you are a friend of young Samways, perhaps I can ask you to allow him to act as my representative and your host. I am needed on the bridge while we are in the Canal, but I expect the ship will reach the Mediterranean safely without our senior cadet being on deck to advise her."

He smiled warmly and Jonathan was glad to see the relief in the Old Man's face as he left the cabin. Ali Bey and his brother-officers were entertained right royally in the passengers' smoking-room, so that, almost before they realised it, *Symondsbury Mote* was slowing to a stop to allow pilots and police to leave her before she started on the last long lap to Southampton Water. She was not calling at any intermediate ports so Jonathan expected no further dangers, but he soon found how wrong he was. On the night before they were due to reach Gibraltar, he was standing close to the taffrail, watching the riven glory of the wake as the green-silver fire of the phosphorescence was thrown about in wild confusion, when a man quietly came into position, one on either side of him, so closely that their elbows ground into his. Less than a mile away on the starboard beam, flashed the light of Aldebaran, the flat-iron shaped island, which is the last land before the Rock appears almost due westerly from it.

Something sharp pricked Jonathan's side, and as he flinched away from it, he felt a similar pain on his other side.

"You will keep quite still if you know what is good for you," the man on the right said in a heavily accented voice. "We are stowaways and no one even knows that we are aboard. They did not miss us at Kubri in the Canal, when we did not go ashore with the rest of our 'police' party. We have waited for this chance for a long time but only to-night have we had the opportunity to meet you quite alone. No, do not move," the man grated in his low, careful voice. "If you do these knives will meet in your heart and, before you have any chance to make an outcry your body will be being tumbled about in that wake of wild water which you have been so greatly admiring."

"What do you want?" Jonathan demanded, doing his best to keep his teeth from chattering in his fear. "How did you know I was here?"

"The last question seems to be of little importance," the second man said, speaking for the first time, "Still you may as well know that we have friends aboard who report your movements to us. We were told just now that you were all alone here in the deserted stern and, as we knew that our chance had at last come, here we are. Yan, tell him what we want from him," he said across the lad's face, speaking to his confederate.

"We demand that document you were given

by von Thurstein a few minutes before he died in the side-alley at Suez," Yan snarled. "We have searched your cabin a dozen times while you were on watch, and we know it is not there, but there are many places in a ship where a seaman can hide things. So—either give us the document or die on our daggers here and now."

Suddenly and to his intense surprise Jonathan found that his crippling fears were all gone—he was still shrinking from those needle-like points touching his skin, but his mind was ice-clear and he was ready to join battle against his captors.

"You seem to be very sure that I have some document or other," he said, carefully keeping his voice ashake as though he was still too terrified to help himself, "but I don't know what it is you are driving at. Who is this German whose name you mentioned?"

"Stop your fooling," the second ruffian snapped, and Jonathan winced as the dagger-point came a little further against his flesh. "We know, and you know, that that man who died in your arms in Suez was von Thurstein; the Red Cormorant as he was once called. He gave you a packet, we know that for we have been shown the oiled-silk wrappings which once held it. It was found in your cabin, slit open and with the papers gone. Where are those papers?"

"So I was right," Jonathan thought, "Cheng Loo *is* a traitor." But that had nothing to do with the matter in hand ; these men were quite capable of killing him at once if he angered them, they would drive home their knives and stab without thinking further about it if he continued to defy them. Aloud, he said quaveringly :

" If you do murder me you won't be any nearer finding the papers, will you ? Once I am dead you will have lost your last chance of ever getting hold of them."

That silenced them for a few pregnant seconds until Yan made the inevitable reply :

" If you are dead then, at least, no one else will have the documents."

Jonathan would have given everything he owned in the world to have known what the Red Cormorant's papers might have contained. It might be political disclosures, military plans, or, more likely, seeing what a mixed crew his assailants were, Egyptians in the Canal, Bedouins at Suez, a Chinaman and now these two beauties, one of whom sounded like a Spaniard and the other like someone from a Balkan country, it could be money or treasure which was cementing them into one organisation. Jonathan knew he must risk everything on his guess being correct—for if it was political or military matters that the papers dealt with, his death would be every whit as advantageous as their recapture of them.

" You'll find that you've wasted a lot of money if you do kill me," he said quietly. " I don't think your partners and pals will thank you for striking such an expensive stroke."

There was a pause which was broken only by the hiss and rush of the small seas being riven by the ship's thrusting hull and the tearing rhythm of the twin propellors, the heart-beat of the whole hurrying fabric of steel, wood and rope.

Aldebaran lighthouse blinked close on the beam, so surprisingly close that Jonathan wondered whether something had gone wrong on the bridge —but he had other and far more immediate worries.

"Where are those papers?" growled the man named Yan. "Stop all this play-acting and answer my question."

Once again there came the suggestive, painful prick in his side, but this time Jonathan was ready for it. Very coolly remembering some of the lessons he had learned from the tough and virile British Police in Palestine, he stepped abruptly back, sure that his assailants were momentarily off their guard. Yan moved first, he slid towards the British youngster only to have his chin meet a fist which felt as though it had been carved out of solid mahogany. The would-be assassin reeled back and in his tumble fouled his companion, who had just started to move in to the attack. Jonathan lost no time; stepping in he uppercut Yan again and as the second man tried to jump clear, drove his left hook into the stout paunch with a force which seemed to sink his fist right up to the wrist in the yielding flesh. By Queensberry rules it was a very foul blow indeed, but there is little time to think of the finer points of boxing when you are facing two armed and desperate criminals and all you have are your knuckles.

Jonathan waited for no more ; spinning on his heel he ran forward along the deck, leaving the steel bulkhead of the Isolation Ward on his left and having the flashing light of Aldebaran close on his right side. *Symondsbury Mote* is what is called a " three-island " ship, that is she has a forecastle, midship superstructure and a poop, and as the lad reached the top of the poop ladder he had to swerve to avoid a collision with someone who had simultaneously reached the top of it from below. To his surprise he saw that it was Cheng Loo and, grasping the Chinaman by his shoulder, Jonathan spun him round and hissed in his ear :

" You'd better join your knife-toting friends," and gave him a mighty kick in the pants which sent the steward stumbling helplessly sternwards. Then, afraid that the pair might be close on his heels, Jonathan fled along the short after well-deck and so reached the midship promenade where, to his infinite comfort, several passengers were still moving about. He lost no time in going to the Captain's quarters where he gasped out his tale of attempted murder, carefully repressing, however, all mention of the Red Cormorant and the missing papers.

Captain Brooks looked at him as though he was not quite sure of his subordinate's sanity, and then, his face set in the severest lines, he snapped out:

"I won't have this sort of thing happening aboard my ship, Samways. If you go about babbling this kind of nonsense you will have the passengers scared stiff, and I'll have you learn that nothing gets a vessel a worse reputation than events like this. I think you are dramatising yourself and I am quite sure there are no stowaways of this sort aboard. Why on earth *should* anyone want to kill a miserable dogsbody of an apprentice even if his father is a Member of Parliament? Let me remind you that M.P.'s are ten-a-penny nowadays. There's no motive for such an attack, the whole thing only exists in your imagination. I warn you to be very careful. my lad."

Jonathan was bitterly regretting his promise to the dying man, but, even at this crisis he could not break his word of honour and so stood silent.

"I'll have a search made for these fictional stowaways of yours, Samways, though I am convinced it's all moonshine. What you say of Cheng Loo is arrant nonsense. I can tell you very very frankly that I'd rather have a decent steward like him than a dozen crazy longshore louts like yourself. Now get out, and if you say a word about this crazy yarn of yours to anyone, to anyone mark you, I'll have your indentures cancelled when we reach home. You're nearly out of your time, so don't mess up your whole life by trying to star as the centre-piece in some weird melodrama that exists only in your own overheated imagination. Cut out reading thrillers, for a change, and try the '*Manual of Seamanship*'."

There was nothing that Jonathan could say to stem the angry tirade of words from his outraged skipper, and, ignorant as Captain Brooks was of the real motives behind these queer happenings, Jonathan had to admit that the Old Man was right. When, next morning the whole ship had been searched from stem to stern-post and there was no sign of any unauthorised passengers being aboard, Jonathan kept very quiet. He wondered how the men had got away until he remembered how close Aldebaran had been when he escaped from the poop, but he decided not to risk a further blasting from the Captain by going to him and stating his opinion of what had happened. For the remainder of the voyage Jonathan was very careful to keep as far away from his commanding officer as he could and to stay out in the wing of the bridge whenever the gold-oak leaves on a cap's peak were on deck.

He saw Cheng Loo a great deal, of course. The pock-marked Chinaman showed not a single sign

"Kicking the dropped pistol into the room, he bent down, grabbed the operator by the shoulders and dragged him within."

of what was passing in his mind, but Jonathan said nothing—there was nothing he could say if he was not to get into further trouble. In due course *Symondsbury Mote* warped herself alongside Southampton quay in the dusk of evening, and, as soon as she had done so, the lad nipped ashore and spoke urgently into the telephone in the call-box, with the result that his father drove all through the night from their West Dorset home and was alongside at crack-of-dawn. Captain Brooks grunted a surly assent when Colonel Samways asked for special leave for his son, and seemed more than glad when Jonathan went ashore with all his gear. He was to go home for a rest, so his father announced, before attending the Navigation School, where he was to spend some weeks studying for his Second Mate's examination. The last person Jonathan saw aboard, after bidding his shipmates in the half-deck farewell, was Cheng Loo, who, wooden-faced as ever, accepted a tip from the colonel for carrying his son's baggage to the waiting car.

But, as soon as they were clear of the docks, Jonathan's father asked him to tell all that had happened since he left Mustafa Effendi's hospitable home that eventful night in Suez.

By the time the lad had finished they were well past the "John Barleycorn Inn" and were speeding through the New Forest towards Ringwood.

"I was extremely interested to learn that you

met the Red Cormorant," the colonel said after his son had ended his tale. "Poor fellow; that was a terrible end for such a man as he. I remember him in his heyday, when he was one of the greatest figures in the Near and Middle East. I recall someone saying, like they did of Captain Muller of the German cruiser *Emden*, in the First World War, that if he was a thorn in our side, at least he was a mighty fine specimen of the genus thorn. Poor chap, what a ghastly end for him, to die like a dog in a dusty gutter in Suez!"

He fell silent for a moment and then, looking across at Jonathan for a moment, his hands steady on the wheel, asked him if he knew what was in the papers he had sent home.

"Not a thing, Dad," the lad replied. "I know, of course, that they are some queer sort of German words written in Arabic characters, but I don't know enough of the language to make a translation."

"They weren't in German, my boy," his father replied. "Von Thurstein was very clever, for he had used old Anglo-Saxon as his medium. That would be to fox anyone who might spot that the letter was not in Arabic, for there are few folks who can read the language of Saxon England of the days before William the Conqueror. It's small wonder that you could not understand it. By the way, that was a clever thing you did—sending it home by post, for you'd certainly have lost it during the voyage if you had tried to hide it anywhere aboard the ship."

"But what *is* it all about, Dad?" Jonathan asked. "It must be mighty important to cause so much of a rumpus."

"It is," the colonel replied, and then said no more until they were clear of Ringwood, the old church to their left drawing astern as they came on to the main road off the by-pass and so faced the bridge. "You see, the Red Cormorant set down the clues to find the cache of jewels and ancient manuscripts which are known as the von Thurstein Hoard."

While they were speeding along towards Wimborne and then past the stone-walled perimeter of the Drax estate, he told his son that the Red Cormorant had once been a very famous archaeologist and Biblical expert in the years between the First and Second World Wars. Just as Lawrence of Arabia had first been a research worker on the ancient sites of the Middle East, so von Thurstein had concentrated on the examination of localities concerned with Old Testament events.

"He had a large private fortune," Colonel Samways went on, "and with it he bought some of the very valuable things he found in his diggings. His collection of ancient jewellery, and particularly of Scriptural manuscripts, was one of the most precious in the world. The strange part of it is that the Nazis never got hold of the collection in the Schloss Thurstein, an old castle in Saxony where the Red Cormorant's family had lived for centuries. The collection vanished into thin air in 1941, for we found among the German archives an account of how Hitler's men had tried to confiscate it while the Red Cormorant was serving them so nobly in the Arab countries. The S.S. men never found a single piece of the collection and, as the Red Cormorant himself disappeared shortly after we marched into Syria, no word has been heard of it since. That is," he corrected himself, "until I had translated the papers you sent me."

Jonathan was fairly bouncing in his seat with excitement. "Then they show the place where he hid all these things ?" he asked.

"No, the Red Cormorant was far too sensible and wary for that. They tell only of where the first clue can be found. He's made the whole thing rather like one of those Treasure Hunt games you play at parties ; his letter merely tells us where to look for the clue to where the Thurstein Hoard is hidden. He says, too, that he has added to its value for it seems that he was the first person to find that hoard of ancient Biblical manuscripts about which there has been so much publicity. You will remember them, Jonathan, some Bedouins found ancient clay jars in a cave near Nebi Musa mosque, at the north-western end of the Dead Sea, which held many Scriptural manuscripts in Hebrew which are several centuries older than any we knew before."

"Yes, I remember reading it in the papers. Weren't we rather done in the eye about them? I mean wasn't it really our property, as they were stolen by the finders while we still held the Palestine Mandate, and so should have come to us?"

"There's no need for us to go into that little argument," his father broke in. "The rights and wrongs of it are beyond us, but it seems that von Thurstein, having discovered them first and unknown to anyone else, took all the better ones away, leaving only those he considered inferior. He says so quite definitely in this letter and if it's true, then there's no reckoning the value of what he's left lying about somewhere in Palestine. It would be a very fine thing if we could only get those for our British experts to examine and publish, wouldn't it? Let alone the historical jewels that were in the Hoard before the War—there were even some from the Hebrew Temple."

Jonathan sat back in astonishment. It seemed that, quite by accident, by a sheer chance, he was involved in the greatest treasure-hunt of recent times, perhaps of all History, for the ancient documents were of the most superlative interest in the world. No small wonder that the opposition (as he mentally called the people who had tried to get the paper from him so violently) were prepared to go to any lengths.

They were still talking about the enthralling subject when they entered Dorchester. The traffic was heavy in the long, narrow street as it was market-day, so that the colonel had to keep his wits about him as he threaded his way through the jumble of cars, buses, lorries, motor horse-boxes and carts. It was approaching nine o'clock and, as they had not breakfasted, they decided to do so at the Antelope Hotel, a fine old Inn in which the rooms used by Judge Jeffreys at the Bloody Assize of 1685, when the men who followed the Duke of Monmouth to Sedgemoor heard their cruel dooms, are still shown.

It was while they were turning off the main road to reach the "Antelope," that Jonathan caught a glimpse of a big, black Buick car, one of the latest models, all shiny chromium-plating, and to his incredulous surprise thought he saw the sallow face of the Chinese steward in the back. The glimpse was so brief, and the idea so fantastic, that he was sure he was mistaken, especially as the big car was being driven by a man dressed as an American Air Force officer who had a lady, wrapped in a mink coat, sitting beside him. It was quite impossible that Cheng Loo could be travelling in such distinguished company. Jonathan grinned to himself for the driver was obviously an officer from one of the American air-bases in the north of England, or, perhaps an attaché from the Embassy in London, who was showing some friends or relations the beauty of the West Country.

Consequently he said nothing about it for he did not wish his father to think he was jumpy and, by the time they had finished the excellent breakfast of kidneys, sausages, tomatoes, eggs and a rasher of bacon that the " Antelope " gave them, Jonathan had completely forgotten the Buick car. But it came back to his memory very forcibly before they had gone many miles, for as they approached the sharp left bend where the modern road to Bridport suddenly diverges from the old Roman road that continues, straight as an arrow towards the mighty mounds of Eggardun Hill's British ramparts, the Buick came speeding out of a gate behind them which led into a coppice.

They were not given a chance, for the big, gleaming car accelerated far faster than the colonel's 10-year-old two-seater. It swished up as they pulled into the left to allow it to pass, and it was then that Jonathan saw he had been right, for, grinning evilly at him through the side-window at the back was the yellow mask of Cheng Loo's face, while the fur-clad lady had disappeared and the " American officer " now had his peaked cap pulled down on to the bridge of his nose, and his face buried to the eyes in the upturned collar of his coat. Two more men were in the back of the car, and as he looked at them horrified, Jonathan recognised the two ruffians who had stood beside him with their dagger-points pricking his ribs that night off Aldebaran !

Before he could shout a word of warning, in fact before he could do anything at all, the khaki-clad officer gave a quick twist to his wheel and the rear of the Buick spun like a live thing to give a mighty side-swipe to the small British car. The Samways' roadster reeled, staggered, lurched and then in a mighty crashing of glass and metal, rolled over the bank, turning two complete somersaults before it came to rest. But by then neither Jonathan nor his father had any interest in what was happening.

CHAPTER 5

SUNK WITHOUT WARNING

Two things saved the lives of Colonel Samways and his son Jonathan that morning on the Bridport-Dorchester road. The first was the steel roof of their old car which took the shock of the somersaults without collapsing. The second piece of luck was the sudden appearance of a cycling club above the rise of the Roman road far above them. The young men and girls of the Saltbury Cycling Rovers had been riding the length of the ancient roadway after breakfasting among the ramparts of Eggardun. They were heading towards their next halt at Dorchester and had just reached the crest above the junction of the ancient with the modern roads when the Buick sent the Samways' car spinning over the low bank.

Naturally they pedalled down the steep slope at breakneck speed and were at the scene of the wreck within a few seconds. But they were not in time to get the number of the big car, and were so concerned with the damaged car spinning in its somersaults that they paid very little attention to the attacker, not realising that it was a " hit-and-run " matter—the brutes had not only failed to give assistance to their victims but were callously hurtling away from the scene of the " accident."

Jonathan came to himself with a terrific headache and some sort of hospital scent filling his nostrils. Rather to his surprise he discovered that he was still in this world, and then his memory slowly returned. He tried to sit up but stopped and groaned at the splitting pain in his head. He raised his hands and found that his head was heavily bandaged, but at that moment a cool, friendly woman's voice came through his mental fog bidding him take things easy and not worry.

" Where's my father ? " he asked. " And where am I ? "

" You are in your own home," the nurse replied. " Your father is in his room and the doctor says he will be all right. Now drink this, like a good fellow."

Jonathan gratefully sipped the cool drink that the nurse held for him and dropped off to sleep as the drug took effect. When he again recovered his senses, the pain in his head was almost gone and he was able to sit up and was told what had happened after their car had come to rest, how the assailants had driven off and the doctor in the ambulance, recognising Colonel Samways, had taken him home rather than to Dorchester hospital.

Later in the morning Jonathan, whose only injury was the rap on his head which they had at first feared might have fractured his skull, was taken to see his father. The colonel was lying flat on his bed, and as Jonathan had been told that his father had two broken thighs and several crushed ribs, he asked no unnecessary questions. The nurse went out after warning the lad not to disturb or excite the patient, but as soon as they were alone Jonathan answered his father's questions and also told him about the people who had been in the Buick.

The colonel lay very quiet as he thought this over and for a moment Jonathan was afraid he had fainted, but was relieved when he saw a faint, but indomitable grin, spreading over his father's teak-like face.

"Jonathan, my lad," he said in a thin but extremely determined tone. "We're going to beat these thugs and get the Red Cormorant's Hoard as well, if it's only to bring those old documents to England for our own chaps to work upon. By glory, we'll do it! Between us, my boy, we'll wipe the noses of this bunch of toughs."

Jonathan's enthusiasm flared at this display of spirit by his father, and as the days passed and his head grew better, he became very anxious to start on the quest. His father, too, was planning and thinking as he lay helpless in the plaster-casts which forbade him any bodily movement. Quietly and thoroughly they discussed plans and the lad was both honoured and very proud that his father, for the first time, treated him as an equal. Many things had to be considered and among the first was the vital need to avoid all publicity.

The colonel decided that it would be fatal to ask for permission to send an expedition to Palestine, for that would not only leak out to the newspapers, but both the Israeli and Arab interests in the Holy Land would, naturally become involved. Between their rivalries the Hoard as they now referred to von Thurstein's treasure, might easily be lost or destroyed. Even more to be avoided was the lead which publicity would give to the gangsters. Their clue pointed to a part of Samaria which lies in the debatable land between the lines of the Israeli forces and those of the Jordan Arab Legion. Both father and son knew the locality intimately, for the Red Cormorant had described a hiding-place in the hills above the Tulkarm-Nablus Road, not far from the village of Kuryet Jett which stands on a famous Old Testament site.

" There's only one way in which you'll stand a chance to reach Palestine in secrecy," the colonel said, looking up into his son's face. " You'll have to go to the Palestine coast in a small craft without anyone knowing that you're aboard her. It will be expensive but I reckon it's worth it."

He then told Jonathan that he would have to make the attempt alone, and so, at least would have no associates who might betray him. His local knowledge of the country and his command of Arabic and Hebrew should make it easier for him to penetrate into that maelstrom of fighting, intrigue and trickery which is the modern state of Palestine.

" You'll find Palestine very different from what you knew, Jonathan," he warned him. " Don't forget that all the coastal areas and quite a lot of the back country is now an independent state recognised by the United Nations. You'll have to keep clear both of the Israelis and also of the Arabs, especially as Kuryet Jett village lies in the No Man's Land between the two areas. If either side knows what you are after they will do their best to get the Hoard for themselves, and they aren't likely to show you much mercy if they catch you trying to get away with it. Now listen," and he began to describe the plans he had made.

Jonathan listened intently and whistled in amazement at the intricacy and cleverness of his father's instructions. It was easy to see that the colonel was a veteran in dealing with human duplicity and well able to fight even the most crooked mind. In the first place he said that he expected the gangsters would burgle his house now that they knew the document must have reached it. To be prepared for that he had made ready, before his son came home, a set of papers which were also written in Arabic characters, but this time in ordinary German, which gave a purely fictitious plan of the Hoard's hiding-place, deep in the Arabian Desert south-east of Akaba, together with a most tempting list of the jewels which were supposed to have been buried in the ancient tomb described in the letter.

" I want the brutes to steal these papers," the colonel chuckled, " so don't get too worried if you happen to hear things that go bump in the night, Jonathan, or queer noises downstairs. Above everything else don't go down to find out who has broken in. I *want* them to find these papers, as when they've done so we'll be free to make the next move—I only hope they do so before the *Symondsbury Mote* is due to sail on her next voyage," he ended anxiously.

" But—— " Jonathan began and stammered his astonishment that the ship should come into the plan.

" Why, of course she does," the colonel replied. " Once we've had our burglary we shall, of course, report it to the police, but we shan't be able to mention the Red Cormorant's document, shall we? That is where you'll come in, for you'll drive straight to Southampton and contact Cheng Loo, the only man in the gang whom we know how to find. You'll try to persuade him to let you have a share in the Hoard and tell him angrily about the way your home was robbed and about the precious paper being stolen. Of course you won't get anything out of him, but he'll be mighty quick in letting his pals know that you've been squealing to him, and also that you're a pretty poor spirited creature who has given up all hope of ever getting the Hoard. That'll unclamp their supervision over us, convince them that we are harmless and, I hope, send them careering off to Saudi Arabia where a hint to some of my old officers, four of whom are now serving in that country, may make things very difficult for them. Meanwhile, once we are clear of that outfit you will be able to concentrate on getting yourself through the Israeli and Jordan lines to Kuryet Jett village. and finding the clue we need. Understand ?" And he lay back, exhausted, but triumphant.

" Why, Dad," Jonathan cried, " you're a genius ! You ought to have lived in Queen Bess's days and fought Walsingham's men ! History might have been different if poor Mary of Scotland had had someone like you."

" She had," his father replied rather grimly. " The trouble was she did not trust her best friends, few of the Stuarts ever did ! However, that's nothing to do with the case. Let's hope we get our burglary committed on us in plenty of time for you to visit the ship and see Cheng Loo. Once that's done, I'll soon have everything ready for you to pick up a small sailing-craft in the Eastern Mediterranean and so make your way secretly to the coasts of Palestine and find the clue to the place where the Hoard is buried."

. . . . .

Jonathan steadied the helm of the 18-ton *Merkhab*, a two-masted lateen-rigged schooner, as the last of the Isle of Ruadh, a few miles off the Syrian coast, sank beneath the sea-rim astern. He chuckled to himself as he recalled what had happened, weeks before, over two thousand miles away, when the burglars had come to his West Dorset home, as had been anticipated. He smiled, too, as he thought of his amusement as he watched them cautiously ransacking the library, not even guessing that he was a witness of every move they made. Cheng Loo was one of those three night-marauders and so it had been almost comic, when, three days after the burglars had found the misleading papers laid ready for them, Jonathan went aboard *Symondsbury Mote* and angrily accosted the slant-eyed steward in his little pantry at the end of the alleyway.

"Why did you burgle my home near Bridport, Cheng Loo?" he demanded, and felt admiration when the Chinaman did not so much as twitch a muscle in his yellow, impassive face. His eyes never flickered, but continued to look inscrutably into those of his questioner.

"Bridport, Mr. Samways?" Cheng Loo answered. "Bridport? I do not understand.

Where is Bridport ? " and he sounded genuinely puzzled. " Why do you say that I was in Bridport ? I can bring plenty people to swear I not leave Southampton since ship arrive."

" Let's cut out all the fooling, Cheng Loo," Jonathan said, acting the desperate youngster to perfection. " If you'll return those papers you stole from my home I'll give you a share in whatever we find. What's more I won't go to the police and lay a charge of burglary against you."

" No understand," Cheng Loo answered blandly, a fixed, expressionless smile on his face. " What papers you want from me ? You wish to see my discharge-book, yes ? "

" You know perfectly well what papers I mean," Jonathan said between his teeth, although inwardly he was deeply amused, and not a little grateful for the fact that this was not a serious matter. But if he was to deceive this Celestial he had to put on a good showing of anxiety and desperation. " The documents that you and your two pals burgled from my father's study the night before last."

The Chinaman's answer took Jonathan completely by surprise, for without saying a word, Cheng Loo turned on his heels, and still without haste, or betraying any signs of anger or resentment, he stalked down the corridor, and to the lad's intense amazement, walked straight to the Purser's office. There he told the increasingly angry Mr. Struthers his story of having been accused of a crime and calmly repeated Jonathan's statement that he had burgled Colonel Samways' house. The Purser turned angrily on the young cadet.

"By Jupiter, Samways, you'll need to make all this good," he snorted. "Cheng Loo's one of the best men I've ever had in my department and I'm not having him upset by any dogsbody of a sea-going wart like you. You'll apologise, right here and now, and also withdraw these absurd charges of yours. Otherwise I'll run you straight up in front of the Captain, and let him deal with you. I know for a fact that Cheng Loo has not been away from the ship for more than a couple of hours at any time since we reached this port."

Things had now gone quite far enough to convince the gang that the Samways were desperate at the loss of the papers and as Jonathan had no wish to become embroiled in any official row with the Old Man he was quite content to leave matters as they stood. So, murmuring an abject apology to the still expressionless Chinese steward, he meekly accepted the Purser's angry lecture and went ashore to climb into the sports two-seater and drive home.

His father had arranged for his son to have a so-called holiday to the Dalmatian Islands and Jonathan, with his small store of money in travellers-cheques, started off quite openly for his vacation. No one in their neighbourhood thought that it was anything out of the ordinary for him to have a holiday, but when Jonathan reached Split, the beautiful seaside city in Jugo-Slavia, he was quickly in contact with Mikor Yurolivan, who had once been one of his father's closest friends when they both were senior officers. Grey-bearded Mikor had, years before, followed a couple of badly-wanted defaulting financiers to Palestine, where he had not only received every help from Colonel Samways, but had stayed in the English officer's home as an honoured guest for the five weeks he remained in the Holy Land while the extradition procedure for his prisoners was being completed.

The Jugo-Slav listened to Jonathan's story very gravely, but he was not told about the Hoard being the collection of the famous Red Cormorant, for von Thurstein's name is still one of magic throughout the Middle East and the Balkans. He understood that the lad was after a store of ancient Scriptural manuscripts which he wished to get out of the Holy Land without the knowledge of either Arab or Israeli authorities and said he would do all he could to help him.

Jonathan had to bring his attention back to more immediate matters and brought his little craft a little closer to the wind as it veered a couple of points. He made out the faint glimmer of the snows crowning Mount Hermon looming faint and far in the distance. The seas were empty—with any luck he would make his landing in plenty of time before the next dawn broke. As the little ship snuggled down on to her new course he recalled the journey down the Adriatic in a small steamer which the Jugo-Slav officer had arranged for him. He landed close to the Turkish port at the mouth of the Orontes where no one had taken any particular notice of the nondescript young sailor who had travelled quietly up to Antioch. In that ancient city he promptly made contact with yet another friend of his father's. George Krikorian, an Armenian merchant who several years before would have lost his wife, family, and his own life if Colonel Samways had not saved all of them by his prompt and kindly action—an action which, by the way, might have cost him his commission if it had ever become known to his own authorities.

"Your father is a great and noble gentleman," the grey-bearded Armenian said to Jonathan when the lad was admitted to his office and had identified himself. "If there is anything I can do for his son, you have only to mention it. I received word to expect you, but I know nothing of what you have in mind. Not that that matters—if the colonel had not chosen to ignore regulations years ago, I should have been sent to a certain country when their political agents in Palestine tried to seize me and my whole family on a trumped-up charge. The British Government which then ruled that unhappy land would have been forced to surrender me on the extradition warrant, for they could not have refused a request in proper legal form. We were arrested and put in prison to await deportation and if your father had not blinked his eyes, we should not be here, happy together in our own home."

Jonathan murmured how glad he was to meet such a friend, and was very grateful when Krikorian arranged his passage to Rhuad Island, which lies off the Syrian coast, and also for a boat and a reliable crew of two who would await him there and see that he landed safely on the coast of Palestine. The two seamen were rough diamonds and both looked extremely formidable and savage, but Jonathan soon found that he need fear no treachery—they were completely and utterly loyal to their Armenian employer in Antioch.

The plan they made was for him to swim ashore after diving overboard as the boat ran down the coast close inshore under sail. She had her papers all in order to land at Haifa a cargo of ropes made in Rhuad and to pick up nails, screws, rivets and other hardware imported from Europe which are essential for the boat-building that is the island's ancient and only industry. Ships have been built on Rhuad since before the days of Cleopatra. Even nowadays most of the little schooners that ply along the shores of the Eastern Mediterranean had their keels laid down on the island's slipways.

The two seamen fully believed that their passenger was an Arab for all their conversation was in that language. Jonathan had also allowed them to gather a vague idea that he was a secret agent for a large commercial combine who wished to learn something about the real strength of the armed forces of the Israeli Army, so that they could decide whether to invest large funds in Israel's future should the prospects appear to justify their taking such a risk. Jonathan, in addition, let them glean that his own special purpose was to gather information for the Staffs of the Arab armies. This pretext had entirely won their friendship, for to men already well disposed towards him because he had been sent by the Armenian, the idea appealed to them that they were also helping a good Moslem to learn the secrets of the hated Israelis, whom they regarded, fiercely and insistently, as foreign and infidel interlopers to be expelled as soon as Allah willed.

"We should be about two hours more," Mohammed Ali, the *Reis*, or skipper of the little craft said later that night as they ran closer inshore. "By that time we should be close to El Zeeb, which is a small plantation north of the walled city of Acre. We thank you for helping us with the steering throughout the day, but perhaps it is now time for you to start your preparations for swimming ashore."

Jonathan agreed, and as he turned to go below asked to be called at once if there was any sign of an Israeli patrol-boat.

" I must learn of such a danger in plenty of time, O most worthy *Reis*," he said, quietly. " Should we sight a ship belonging to the Forgotten of Allah," using the name the Arabs employ when they mean an Israeli, " it will be better for all of us if I dive overboard. If I am caught aboard your ship it may mean, besides a firing-squad for me, a life-time in jail for both of you. Therefore give me plenty of warning."

Reis Mohammed Ali grinned and replied that he would give his passenger plenty of time to escape over the side should there be a patrol at sea that night, and, comfortable in this assurance, Jonathan went below to make ready his gear. He packed the scanty garments of a Jewish farm-worker into a waterproof bag ; made sure that he had the few pounds of Israeli money that the Armenian merchant had given him, and then, stripping off his Arab clothes, he lay down on the narrow bunk to wait for the call to dive overboard as they passed El Zeeb.

Jonathan, tired with his day in the open, must have dozed off for he heard no cry of warning before there was a terrific explosion, a sheet of searing flame and the air seemed filled with the whining of metal fragments. The little ship lurched, staggered, lay over to one side, and then, as the water poured in through her torn side, Jonathan, who had meanwhile slid to his feet, felt her diving beneath his feet towards the sandy floor of the Mediterranean. As he tried to swing himself up on deck, a crashing cascade of water poured down the narrow hatchway, sweeping him back as helplessly as a drowning rat.

All was confusion, noise, creaking, cracking of wood and the wild inrush of roaring water, as the little ship stood steeply on her stern-post and, with ever-increasing acceleration, slid away from under him. To make bad infinitely worse, a second bright flash, followed by the whipping crack of a bursting shell, once more tore the night, and, even as the vessel dived, her disappearing hull was riven and gashed by the shrieking splinters of the shell.

Jonathan, holding tight to the table, dragged himself toward the hatchway, and fighting desperately against the torrent of salt water, tried to force his body out into the open. With the speed of a lift, she dived ; the darkness closed in, the sea rushed into his face, and, torn from his hold, he felt himself spinning as helplessly as a cork in a mill-race. The thought flashed through his mind that the search for the Red Cormorant's Hoard was finished so far as he, personally, was concerned, almost before it had begun.

CHAPTER 6

THE PIRATE'S BASE

JONATHAN'S only recollections of the few seconds that followed the crash of the second shell were of being thrown helplessly about ; of an agonising crash into something hard and then an agony in his shin as the skin was scraped from it a second before he was suddenly freed of obstructions and twirling in rushing water. He had been washed out of the little cabin, ejected through the hatchway in the mad swirl of water and air and was now a few feet to one side of the vessel as she plunged into her deep grave.

His downward course continued, he felt that something alive, malignant and brutal was dragging him towards the sea-floor. Suddenly the tearing drag ceased and changed to an upward soaring at an incredible speed, but the surface seemed to be such measureless miles away that he quite despaired of reaching it before his lips would be forced open to suck in the killing draught of salt-water that would flood his lungs and kill him. Then, without his quite knowing how it had happened, his head was thrust above the surface with such velocity as he shot from the depths that he came clear nearly as far as his waist, before he fell back again, automatically treading water as any animal will instinctively do if it falls into a river.

Gratefully he gulped deep breaths of the cool, fresh night-air, while all around his head there were splashings as parts of the sailing-craft hurtled up from below, often rising clear from the surface only to fall back again threatening him with death and injury from their cruel weight as they did so. Then, as he recovered sufficiently to notice what was happening, he became aware of a large, dark shape moving across the sea—and realised that this must be the craft which had so treacherously and wantonly destroyed his little ship. There was a deep hum and throb of motor-engines as it drew nearer to allow him to hear the sound of voices after the shadow suddenly altered her course and cruised slowly towards him.

He wondered, anxiously, what flag she wore. If she was an Israeli Navy gunboat she was not likely to be very hospitable to survivors of a Syrian ship she had sunk, while it was trying to sneak down their coast. The thought then arose that an Israeli warship was not at all likely to fire without warning—after all their Government was recognised by nearly all the States of the world and they would never carry out such piratical tactics. In any case her officers would be far more anxious to establish the identity of so mysterious an intruder than to destroy any chance of ever finding out who she was.

He next learned that she did not belong to the new State, for the men on her forecastle were speaking in Arabic. Filled with such sudden and unreasoning relief that he lost all caution, Jonathan hailed them in the same language, and heard their startled exclamations at finding anyone still alive. A moment later her twin-screws threshed as they were put working hard-astern and as she stopped he found himself bobbing alongside a little ship which looked very like one of the motor-launches used by the Royal Navy in the Second World War.

A line splashed on to the water beside him and in a strangely-accented Arabic, which he recognised as that of the Turkish border to the northwards, he was bidden make himself fast in the noose of the running-bowline at its end. A moment later, his chest squeezed agonizingly tight by the snatch of the rope, he was hauled aboard and lay gasping on the deck just forward of the low bridge. Someone released the painful rope and then he was dragged to his feet to face several dimly visible men.

" By Allah's self, but the man is mother-naked. He wears no clothes," a mocking voice said.

" Take him below. I will interrogate him in my cabin. Quick, those devils ashore are already stirring. Full speed ahead on both engines. I see a searchlight being started up."

Engineroom-telegraph bells jangled and the vessel hummed into life as the man who had given the command to take Jonathan below, ordered the helm to be jammed hard-down. The two men beside the rescued youngster pulled at his arms and with snarling voices bade him descend the ladder if he wished to avoid being thrown down it like a sack of potatoes. Dazed, and feeling wretchedly sick and ill, Jonathan turned to obey just as a bright sword of light sprang up from the distant shore, and, almost simultaneously, two guns fired from the old city of St. John of Acre, whose ancient walls have their feet in the sea.

Instantly all was confusion aboard the boat and her speed accelerated sharply, so sharply indeed that Jonathan saw he had been mistaken in taking her for an old M.L. sold out of the Royal Navy, and knew that she must have been a motor-torpedo boat, or perhaps a speedy E-boat which had once belonged to Hitler's forces. The little ship raised her bow in the air and the last glimpse that Jonathan had of anything outboard before he went through the hatch and down the ladder, was of a great bow-wave creaming like snow, gleaming with phosphorescence as it roared away from the step abreast the bridge.

The whole vessel was humming with her great speed and the full thrust of her powerful engines as he stood, waiting, in the narrow alleyway at the foot of the ladder with his two captors standing grimly beside him. Electric lights were burning brightly in the passage showing him that his guards were a villainous looking pair of Levantines, who might have been Arabs, Turks, Greeks or any one of the numerous communities who live along the eastern edges of the Mediterranean. They were staring at him with the greatest interest and, for the first time, Jonathan grew conscious that he was completely nude.

" This looks as though we have made an important capture, Idris," said the man standing at his left side. " Look at him, this is no Syrian nor man of Palestine. His skin is white below the sunburn-line of his neck. He is a Frank," by which term Europeans are known in that part of the world.

" Maybe he is one of the Forgotten of Allah," the other man nodded. " Whoever he is the captain will be glad to question him, and he'll not take long to discover who he is. Listen, can't you hear the fall of shells? The Jews are daring to fire upon us, and by the sound of the bursts they are making good practice. That last one was not one hundred metres on our starboard quarter."

" They have good cause," his shipmate replied with a chuckle. " I reckon that we have given them more trouble than anyone else who has yet tried to keep the Shrines of Jerusalem from being profaned. But they will never hit us—the range is too great and you can feel how the captain is throwing the ship around."

They both laughed as they steadied themselves against a quick and savage turn which almost put the ship on her beam-ends as the fast craft's helm was thrust hard-over. For some minutes this mad listing and careening went on, Jonathan finding it very hard to keep his balance in the wild twistings and writhings as the ship was driven through the curtain of gunfire from the shore, but, after about a quarter of an hour or so, she settled down on to a steady course and her speed was also cut down to, so far as he could judge, an economical twenty knots or so.

Feet rattled down the after-ladder a few seconds later, and a man wearing a hard-weather cap, his face half hidden in a silk muffler and with a pair of powerful night-glasses dangling from a strap around his neck, entered the alley-way from the door opening into the forward tankroom. He looked at the little group and then stepped into a cabin on the starboard-side, bidding the two seamen bring in the prisoner.

Jonathan was hustled roughly through the doorway to face the captain who had seated himself on a leather-covered broadside settee. The two seamen drew back and he found himself looking into one of the most brutal faces which he had ever had the ill fortune to see. The sabre-scars on the flat, grey cheeks indicated that the man was probably a German, the product of some University, or, more likely, a Prussian naval officer of the old school. That thought made Jonathan look more closely and he realised that despite his leanness and the smoothness of his skin, the captain was a man in his later fifties. But it was the cold, grey, hectoring, intolerant eyes that struck real fear into the lad's heart—this man was evil, a cold-blooded, impersonal "killer" the sort of sadistic brute who might have been one of the Nazis' concentration-camp commandants. But Jonathan had only a few seconds for his study of the man who had sunk his little ship, for the captain spoke in a harsh, rasping voice, in an Arabic that was heavily accented in the fashion which the Germans use.

"Who are you?" he demanded, looking at the naked lad. "Do not lie. I can see by the colour of your hide that you are no Arab. To me you appear to be a Northern European. Are you English or Scandinavian?"

Inspiration flashed into Jonathan's mind, he would tell half the truth.

"I am English," he admitted and fell into fiction. "I am a special reporter for a British newspaper that wants to learn the real inside story of what is happening in Palestine. I speak good Arabic because I was born in Jerusalem, where my father was a senior official in the Mandatory Government. My newspaper thought it was a good idea to have a good story about the inside of events in Palestine, as people are bored with the yarns that they are getting from official Jewish and Arab sources."

"What was your father's name and department?" the man snapped.

Jonathan gave the name of a man who had been a senior in the Lands Department, but who had died after returning to England.

"James Armstrong," he replied. "My name is Walter Armstrong," and then he thought it was high time to put on a show of indignation at the outrage he had suffered, and taking a half-step forward he raged:

"Never mind all this question-and-answer stuff. What I want to know is who you are and by what authority you sank my ship, killed my men and now make me stand before you. Who the devil are you, anyway?"

The man took not the slightest notice of this tirade but drew a blue-covered book from the shelf above his head and Jonathan thanked his lucky stars that he had used the name of a real man, for beneath the royal cypher of Great Britain, he read the words in gilt letters, "Government of Palestine—Staff List."

"Armstrong," the man read aloud, speaking in English. "Supervisor of Registrations, Land Department. Grade 2, Senior Service." He looked up at his prisoner. "Well, you seem to have spoken the truth," he remarked, although his grim, grey eyes never flickered. " Hmm, we must now see what it is best to do with you, my friend, but that cannot be decided until we return to base. Meanwhile," and he spoke a few words in his bad Arabic to the two seamen, bidding them get some clothes for the castaway.

Jonathan spluttered a demand for an apology but was met by an icy evil stare, and when he persisted, the German waved an impatient hand, whereupon the two seamen, none too gently, dragged him out of the cabin. Jonathan submitted after pretending to make a futile struggle, and quietly accepted the khaki drill trousers and a grey cotton shirt that were brought to him from the forecastle. As soon as he was clad he was led aft along the deck and told to jump down into the tiller-flat, which he did, after catching a short glimpse of the hurrying seas, white-capped from the boat's swift progress, that were dashing away into the night.

It was very dark and smelly down in the reeling tiller flat where the twin-screw immediately beneath it kept up a monotonous drumming and rumbling that was intensified by the banging and squealing of the steering-gear. Being right aft he felt her pitching very severely, but he was seaman enough not to be worried about that until, to his own surprise, the steady monotony of sound around his ears, sent him off into a deep sleep.

He awoke feeling as though his mouth was filled with old brass-screws for the atmosphere in the dark, unventilated compartment was very foul. The engines were turning more slowly, it was probably their altered rhythm that had wakened him, and through the half-secured steel deadlight over a dirty, paint-splashed scuttle, he saw that it was broad daylight outside. He staggered to his feet attracted by the glimmer of light and saw that they were passing close beside some high, rocky land whose grey, boulder-strewn slopes were broken only by a few stunted wild-olive trees and some sparse scrub.

A white-walled, red-tiled house came into sight and, a few seconds later, the view was blotted out by a stone wall a few inches from the dirty glass as the boat drew alongside a wharf or mole. The incessant squealings and bangings died away as the engines stopped and the helm was abandoned, but a considerable time elapsed before anything happened so far as he was concerned. It grew very warm down in the tiller-flat as the sun beat down on the deck above with no cool wind flowing over it to temper its heat, so that Jonathan was both thirsty and very nearly exhausted with excessive perspiration before footsteps drummed overhead and the steel hatch banged back to reveal a circular patch of blue sky. That was quickly half-obscured by the shape of a man's head, who snarled a command for him to come upon deck.

Jonathan was only too glad to obey and staggered up the steep steel rungs on to the deck. Only to wince as his bare feet met the sun-smitten planking. Looking interestedly he saw at once that the ship was an old German E-boat, or, rather, to use their proper title, an S-boat, which the Nazi Navy used as we did our M.T.B.'s. It had been re-armed, for though it still had its torpedo-tubes, the gun on the forecastle was a much larger one than any S-boat had carried during the war, probably a 4-inch, he judged.

A village stood close to the head of the jetty alongside which they lay, a collection of small houses clinging to the rocky mountainside. The harbour looked more like the crater of some small extinct volcano than anything else, its only entrance a narrow gap in the all-surrounding cliffs through which he saw a tiny segment of the sea beyond. On the far side of the little pier was another boat of about their own size, one of the Harbour Defence motor launches, H.D.M.L.'s they were called, which were once used in the Royal Navy of His Brittanic Majesty, King George VI.

He was given very little time to look around, however, before his escorts gruffly bade him follow them ashore, but here Jonathan decided to play awkward, and, sitting down on the coaming of the S-boat's after-hatch, he stated very definitely that he was not going to walk an inch along that uncomfortably hot jetty without something to protect his feet.

" You can carry me if you like," he said, defiantly. " Or you can save yourselves a lot of trouble by finding me a pair of shoes. Please yourselves, for I'm not walking barefoot, and I'll fight as long as I can stand before you'll make me do so."

After some grumbling and growling of threats the man in charge of the party seemed to think it might be less troublesome if they acceded to his prisoner's demand, and growled a command for the third seaman to jump below and see what he could find. When the man returned carrying a pair of old rope-soled canvas shoes, grey with neglect and age, Jonathan tried them on and, finding that they were wearable, although a size or so too large, he rose to his feet and bade them lead on.

He was most anxious to discover what sort of an organisation he had fallen among, for he wanted time to prepare his counter-measures. The sinister, middle-aged German ex-officer, the polyglot crew, the armed S-boat, the sinking of the schooner so close to the Palestine coast, all proved that he was the prisoner of some sinister gang of pirates, but, guess as hard as he liked, he could not reach the least conclusion as to who, or what, organisation might be behind them.

The coast of the Levant, lying between the

borders of Egypt and Turkey, was a prey to lawlessness and to war, and with the Royal Navy no longer maintaining its patrols, an ideal place for piracy. Piracy may be thought obsolete yet it crops up at once in any part of the world as soon as a strong naval power no longer keeps the peace. If these toughs were pirates, Jonathan reflected, he would be in a very dangerous situation, for they would certainly take every precaution to prevent him from betraying their activities and their base.

The village, too, was a strange silent place, for he quickly learned that there was not a woman or a child among its few houses. Tales of villages in the Grecian Archipelago which had been emptied by the Germans and never reoccupied because all their former inhabitants were dead came to his mind. There were plenty of signs, however, that the people who now lived in it considered themselves to be at war, for there were several guns mounted to cover the entrance to the harbour, while at least four parties were lounging near anti-aircraft pieces, whose lean muzzles were pointing to the bright blue of the sun-smitten sky.

Jonathan heard the whine of a radio-transmitter as well as the hum of a dynamo higher up the hill, and he passed a small party of men working on a dam across a small, swiftly-flowing stream that flowed down one side of the village. But he did not have very much time to make any fuller observation, for his three guards hustled him swiftly along until they reached a strange building which clung to the cliff-side like a house-martin's nest to the wall of a building. Jonathan had seen these strange rock-monasteries before, there are several of them in Palestine, so that he was not too surprised when he found himself led into a long, vaulted chamber, half-masonry, half rock-hewn, which, with its long stone-tables, must have been the refectory of the monks in the days before the Germans drove them out along with the rest of the inhabitants.

As his eyes became more accustomed to the cool dimness of the old chamber he saw more clearly the faces of the three men who were sitting on the far side of the Abbot's table, and a sudden terror flooded him, for the man in the middle was an Arab leader who had been known to everyone in Palestine as one of the bitterest fanatics of his race. Haj Yussef was still wearing the black, cassock-like garment and the snow-white *laffi* bound turban-wise round his scarlet fez that had been his distinguishing habit when he was one of the chief leaders of the Moslems in Jerusalem. Fortunately Jonathan's involuntary start passed unnoticed, while the pallor draining the colour from his face was concealed by the fact that he was standing with his back to the bright light coming through the refectory door. Taking what comfort he could from the fact that the Haj might not recognise in the stalwart young man standing before him someone whom he had last seen as the 12-year old son of a senior police officer, Jonathan recovered his composure and faced his captors with a well-acted display of anger.

"I do not begin to understand why you are treating me as a prisoner," he began in Arabic, speaking indignantly before they had any chance to say a word. "You wantonly blow my ship out of the water, you stow me away in a filthy tiller-flat without refreshment or ventilation, and then you have me marched up here like a common thief. I demand——"

"Silence!" snarled the Prussian, his face livid with rage. "If you wish to live you will keep a civil tongue in your head and also give us some good reason why we should not rub you out as a useless nuisance."

The German turned to the man sitting on the far side of Haj Yussef and for the first time Jonathan had a chance to look at his third judge. He was a shrivelled, very aged man, and, like the Haj, wore the habit of a Moslem religious dignitary.

"Most holy Lord and Caliph," the Prussian said, in a mock-humble voice. "You now see the young Frank whom I took from the sea off the coast of Acre. Because of the fact that I saw he was neither Arab nor Jew but a European, I did not throw him back into the water, but brought him here in case he might have something of interest to tell us. Will you deign to question him, or shall someone else do so on Your Nobility's behalf ? "

The old man moved his toothless gums and his sparse white beard jigged for a few seconds as he cackled in his dry and toneless voice that he had no wish to speak to an infidel, and expected that the Haj, too, would not wish so to demean himself. He then bade the German, whom he called Reis Ahmet, to go ahead. The Arab name made Jonathan look again at the German ; there have been plenty of cases throughout the ages of sailors who have turned renegade, taken Mohammedan names, and fought on the seas against their own kind.

The Prussian-Moslem humbly thanked the old man and then, still speaking in Arabic, began to deliver a long speech. In it he avowed that he was waging war against the Israeli State in defence of the Holy Cause of the Faith, and that it had been in the course of their blockade that the sailing-vessel had been destroyed by gunfire. Haj Yussef nodded his venerable-looking head in complete agreement, and broke in at this point to remark that if Moslem seafarers had not the piety and loyalty to cease trading with the enemy of their Religion, then True Believers must make it their business to see that they did, even if it meant the death of unworthy brethren in the Faith.

Jonathan began to wonder why he was being

treated to this long talk but the Prussian's next words showed him the reason for it all. They believed that their prisoner really was a newspaper's special correspondent, and were trying to win his support for what they were doing.

" We wish you to write favourably of our holy Cause in your paper," the Prussian said. " If you will extol the fervour of Islam and say that not every Moslem has retreated from his plain duty to check the growth of these Jews in Israel, it will focus attention that all is not quite so peaceful as the Western World has been led to believe. We need help in our war against the Forgotten of God."

" If I do refuse to write because I think that what you are doing is sheer piracy, what will happen ? " Jonathan asked, and could have kicked himself for his clumsy question.

" It seems, my friend, that you have already taken extraordinary pains to disappear into the dark underground of this part of the world in order to reach Palestine secretly," the Prussian said, with a smile that was very dreadful and sinister. " So, if you will not be our friend and might indeed become our enemy, no one will ever be certain at what stage of your journey you finally became entirely lost to the sight of man."

Jonathan's heart missed a beat—there could be no doubt of the man's fixed purpose to blot out any bar to the success of his plans.

" Very well, then," the lad went on in a voice that cost him a superhuman effort to make casual, " what do I get if I write this article you require? I don't see how I can do so without revealing your secret base and then you will soon have warships round to smoke you out as pirates."

" That is also true," Haj Yussef broke in, " but as we shall await a suitable date for sending your writings to your editor we will be free to choose a time when it can do us no harm, your objection will not matter. Perhaps, indeed, we shall not be able to use you at all, and then we shall have to decide your fate. Meanwhile, you will write your article and wait."

" Then what happens to me? " Jonathan asked. " You have no guarantee that once I have left the island I shall not speak about what I have seen."

" Precisely," said the Prussian, and now all sign of a smile had faded from his face. " Mr. Armstrong, you will be our guest here on Skanthos Island until we decide either that it is safe to let you go, or take other measures to ensure your silence. The only thing that you may exercise any choice about, is the fashion of your hospitality. Show yourself friendly by doing as we ask and we shall allow you to be comfortable. But, to make quite sure that you will not be able to denounce us later on, we may eventually take you to sea in our ships to help in the destruction of all shipping we can catch off the infidel coast and so make you our accomplice. If you refuse, however, to show yourself our friend, then, I am desolated to say, you must consider being left to die, as quickly as you can, in one of the dungeons of this monastery, or, perhaps, walled-up in one of the many rock-tombs which dot the mountainside above us."

Suddenly his voice changed to a whip-lash of command.

"Which is it to be? Do you write what we require, or do you choose to die? We have no more time to waste on you. There is other and more important work claiming the time of this Council of the Brotherhood."

Chapter 7

THE PIRATES PUT TO SEA

Jonathan shrugged his shoulders.

"You don't offer me much of a choice, do you?" he said, sarcastically, and then added, "Well, I don't suppose it matters. I've no reason to be in love with the Israeli Government, so I can't see that I'll do my conscience much of an injury by giving you a hand. It may even make a book sometime in the years ahead. But if it's going to be up to the standard my editor requires I'll need a little time to do the writing. It can't be done in a blind hurry."

The German glowered at him, and Jonathan knew that cold-blooded murder lay close to the surface of those cruel eyes. If it had not been for the old man whom they called the Caliph, and also for Haj Yussef's idea that the young Briton might yet be useful, he would have been killed and no one in the outside world would ever learn what had happened to him. Jonathan had not the least illusion about his personal danger as he stood there facing the three strange men on the far side of the long-dead Abbot's dining-table, but he allowed no sign of what he was thinking to show on the surface.

The German growled an order to the seamen that the young guest was to be allowed the liberty of the village but, if they ever had the slightest reason to believe that he was trying to escape, they were to seize him at once, and, no matter what the hour of day or night might be, to bring him up for sentence. Scarcely daring to believe in this respite, Jonathan thought it was time to appear more at his ease, and, rather truculently, asked for better clothing and more suitable footwear.

" That will be attended to," the German replied, ungraciously. " Go to Giacomo Baldini ; you'll find him at the first house at the head of the jetty. He'll fit you out. Meanwhile, my friend, I warn you to be very careful not to do anything we may not like. Take him away."

The seamen saluted as though they had been serving in a Royal Naval base, one of the first signs Jonathan noted that discipline among these pirates was sternly maintained, and one of them tapped him on the shoulder and turned away. Jonathan drew a great breath of relief when he emerged from the doorway of the half-ruined monastery and felt the bright sun and the fresh wind from off the sea blowing over him. His escort left him on the terrace outside and he turned down the step-like street towards the store-house of Baldini which he reached without further incident.

Baldini was one of those red-headed Italians from the north, and was probably of Tyrolian ancestry, for no one more unlike the ordinary Italian whom one pictures could have been met in a day's march. He was a giant of a man and, like so many big men, was filled with a heartiness which, however, did not conceal the innate evil which had brought him down to becoming a renegade serving in a pirate-base. He had not the least misgivings about talking over things that most men would have been only too glad to hide as a shameful secret.

While he gave the lad the clothes and footwear he needed, Baldini regaled him with bloodcurdling yarns about things that had happened along the coasts of Syria and Palestine in recent years. By his own account he had been in the Italian Navy during the war when he had served in the Suicide Squads of frogmen who made the daring raids which sank the British battleships *Queen Elizabeth* and *Valiant* in Alexandria. He gloried in stories of what he had done after returning to Italy, where he was one of the extermination-squad whom Mussolini had employed to silence some of his most dreaded opponents in his abortive Northern Republic. He also explained that it was because he was so badly wanted for several of these killings in his own country that he had joined the Moslem Faith and was now an officer in the Brotherhood of the Steel Crescent, as, so he vaingloriously entitled the gang of pirates, who were waging a private war against the people of the new State of Israel, styled themselves.

During the next three days Jonathan saw a lot of Baldini, although he knew he was playing with something just about as dangerous as an atomic bomb. He listened carefully to the red-headed Italian giant's stories, and, by carefully flattering him, learned a great deal. On the fourth day of his imprisonment Jonathan completed a long and lurid article, addressed to the editor of a London newspaper, in which he lauded these new corsairs of the Mediterranean to the skies. The German wallowed in all this romantic nonsense of being called a twentieth century edition of the famous renegade Barbary Corsair, Kheir-ed-Din Barbarossa, who was the scourge of the Inland Sea in the days when Tudors sat on the throne of Britain.

Jonathan was only too well aware that he was sitting on the top of a volcano which might erupt violently at any moment, while added to his constant peril was his need to get on with his quest for the Red Cormorant's clue to the Hoard. If he did not show up fairly soon his father might commence inquiries which would betray the fact that his son had left for Palestine. At all costs, he must escape from the Isle of Skanthos before the Prussian captain discovered that his tale of being a newspaper-correspondent was false;

Jonathan had not the least illusion as to what would happen to him if it was ever established that he had lied about himself.

No one seemed to take much open interest in his movements, but he soon discovered that he was not going to be permitted to quit the village for, twice, when he had tried to walk casually up the rock-strewn mountainside, a couple of men appeared from behind big boulders and gruffly ordered him back. At nightfall he was shut inside one of the small cottages where he quickly discovered that one of the look-out men at the jetty always kept a fairly vigilant eye on his door. He saw nothing of the German captain but the skipper of the old H.D.M.L. proved more friendly. He was an American and frankly admitted that he was a soldier-of-fortune who could not go home because the Federal police were interested in him.

He yarned quite freely with Jonathan and suggested that the British youngster might do much worse than join the Brotherhood, saying that he could find room aboard his craft for a competent second-in-command.

"After all, it's not so bad," he said on Jonathan's third evening in Skanthos. "We're only doing what people like Francis Drake or Harry Morgan got British knighthoods for doing. The pay's good and the Crescent of Steel people treat you decently; after all, they've got a real grievance, or think they have, about the new political set-up in this part of the world. They honestly believe that they have the right to blockade the Palestine coast and, as they aren't seamen enough to do it for themselves, they pay queer birds like our Kraut friend and me to do it for them. Come on in with us, you'll never regret it."

But Jonathan saw only too clearly that it was a purely criminal set-up—the brutal murder of the two men who had been taking him to the shores of the Holy Land was proof enough of that. Beneath the easy exterior of the American ex-naval officer he sensed the true brutality of the man and he knew that Jan Smithers as he called himself, would be absolutely ruthless in his dealings with any man or woman who was unlucky enough to get in his way. The American's callous talk made him even more afraid than did the open brutality and arrogance of his German fellow-captain.

On the fourth morning, there was sudden and intense activity in Skanthos. Both boats began to make ready for sea and Jonathan received a message from the German that he was to sail that evening as one of the S-boat's crew. During the afternoon rumours began to circulate that the biggest stroke that the pirates had yet tried was to be attempted—they were to sink a big 17,000-ton oil-tanker which was carrying crude-oil from South America to the Haifa refineries, in an effort to restart work there. The pipe-lines from Iraq had been dry for years, as the Arabs of that country refused to allow any fuel to flow down to Israel, while the Egyptians had closed the Suez Canal against any tankers bringing in oil from the south. The Brotherhood of the Crescent of Steel were determined to stop this attempt to bring the badly-needed fuel at all costs, and had ordered their two boats to sea to sink the tanker that was bringing it.

Jonathan heard the men discussing the radio-signals which were coming in to the house on the cliff where the pirates had their station. The messages showed that there were plenty of people outside Skanthos who were extremely anxious to make sure that the ship never reached Haifa. Position-signals were plotted by the American and the German captains who also carefully calculated the exact point where they could ambush the second night after their ships left Skanthos. The British lad was desperate, for although he saw that his best chance of escape would be while the two boats were absent, he had to warn the tanker about the death which lurked for them as they approached the coast of the Holy Land.

It seemed impossible to warn the ship, for it would be very difficult for him to enter the radio station even if he avoided sailing in the S-boat. Even if he reached the transmitter his signal might be heard by the pirates and bring the boats tearing back in a frenzy of murderous rage to destroy the man who had betrayed them. The little house where the transmitter was housed was not particularly well guarded but there were generally at least three hefty ruffians up there, while its front doors and windows were in plain sight of the rest of the village. That point, however, was something that could wait, as he dared not despatch any signal for at least twenty-four hours after the pirate-vessels had left the harbour. What was urgent was that he must hide in some place where they were not likely to find him.

It would be fatal if he was missed before it was time for him to go aboard. If he could only wait until the last moment and then disappear they would not be able to hang about very long to find him for fear of missing their ambush for the tanker. Jonathan took his full share in the labour of carrying stores aboard the ships and helping to water and refuel them, all of which had to be done by hand, the petrol being carried in four-gallon cans from the storehouse at the end of the jetty, the water from the stream tumbling into the little harbour, in similar receptacles.

It was extremely hard and tiring work in the hot sun and, several times, Jonathan saw that the two skippers were noticing and approving his industry. In fact the German halted once as the lad walked past him with a four-gallon can of water hanging from each end of the wooden yoke that he was carrying on his shoulders, and growled something about not being late when the time came to cast off and put out to sea.

"Don't worry, sir," Jonathan replied, setting down his tins and mopping his sweating face. "I'm a journalist and I'd give my right ear for a chance to be able to write up this business for my paper, and the book I'll put together some day."

The German came perilously near to what, on his battle-scarred and weather-marred face, would have been a smile and, with some of his suspicions lulled, went on to his ship. But as the darkness of early evening settled in, Jonathan found jobs that kept him away from the quayside for as long as possible between his visits aboard. It cost a considerable effort in cool nerve for him to go aboard and walk aft, showing himself in the glow from the wheelhouse-door, and to pretend to be busy with a coil of rope aft. The German saw him but said nothing, and so far as Jonathan could tell, had no suspicion that his prisoner had not the least intention of being aboard when the ship sailed.

The last time Jonathan went aboard the S-boat, however, he turned round as soon as he was out of the beam of light from the wheelhouse door, and walking quickly along the other side of the upper deck, crossed the forecastle and jumped back on to the quay. He had one really bad moment when he almost bumped into the American skipper who was just stepping on to the short brow connecting the S-boat with the shore.

" All set, Armstrong ? " the skipper of the H.D.M.L. asked, jovially. " I reckon that this stunt is going to be as big a show as we used to do in the old days when the P.T. boats got into a Japanese convoy. I'm sure looking forward to it, and I guess you're feeling the same way, aren't you?"

" Roaring to go, sir," Jonathan replied with a laugh. " I've got to go to my quarters and collect some personal gear of mine, and then I'll be staying aboard as there doesn't seem to be any more work that needs doing before we cast off."

" Don't be late," the American said with a chuckle. " This is the biggest thing we've yet tried. The tanker ought to be a sitting target for the Kraut's torpedoes, while I'll knock out her aerials and radio-room with my twin 6-pounders. She's cold meat, and the workmen in Haifa refineries are going to be drawing their unemployment pay for quite a while yet, believe me."

Jonathan, anxious to cut short the conversation before the German captain came on deck, said that he really would have to get along if he was to bring any sea-clothes for himself.

" Tell you what," said the American. " I'll ask if you can sail in my craft. You'll find her more friendly than this Jerry-commander's S-boat. What do you say ? "

" That's awfully good of you, sir," Jonathan

replied, infusing a pretence of great warmness into his voice. " I'd love to sail with you and not have to go with Reis Ahmet." The germ of a new idea blossomed in his mind. " However, you'll be casting off very soon, won't you ? Aren't you sailing before Reis Ahmet ? "

" All the more reason for you to hurry," the American grunted. " I'm casting off in ten minutes, but I'll tell him that you're coming with me. You'd better be on time, though, otherwise you'll find yourself learning what a German seaman had to put up with from his Prussian officers. He's a cold-blooded devil to his crew when he's on operations."

" I'll be back in time," Jonathan said, hastily. " But if I am held back, for there's no saying what old Haj Yussef may do in the way of delaying me if I'm unlucky enough to bump into him, will you hang on a few minutes to allow me to come aboard ? "

" Not one single second," the skipper of the ex-H.D.M.L. replied. " Orders are orders and I'm not getting foul of our German friend right at the commencement of things. He's the senior officer and I'm not making an enemy of him over a blasted passenger like you. Be on time, my lad, or you'll make the passage in the S-boat. That's all ! " and turning on his heel, he stamped away towards the German's craft to tell him of the new arrangements he had made.

But Jonathan, with the new and exciting hope of being left behind without either captain suspecting that he had done so deliberately, was speeding up the village street, passing several members of the American's crew who were on their way to go aboard. He had long ago decided on the best hiding-place to spend the twenty-four hours while he was waiting for his chance to despatch the radio-signal that might save the tanker and the eighty-odd men who formed her crew—the old monastery, the headquarters of the bloodthirsty Brotherhood, would be the very last place in which they would expect to find him.

His only real difficulty was to get through its doors without being seen. These stood at the end of a narrow ledge on the face of the cliff, a ledge which had been cut away a few feet from the door-sill, so that there was a gap which dropped three hundred feet to the sea-laved foot of the rock on which it was built. A drawbridge spanned this gap as a defence against intruders and, in ancient days, had probably saved the lives of the monks on more than one occasion when Turkish rovers entered the little harbour.

Jonathan turned off the village-street and walked along the ledge which was about six feet in breadth, watching the activity going on down at the jetty where the last preparations were being made to get the boats away. Lights were flaring down there with the figures of hurrying men outlined against their glare as they bustled about their last-minute tasks. Jonathan, ready to strike hard at any one who might try to stop him, or to overpower any guard who might afterwards report having seen him entering the monastery, found to his surprise that there was no sentry at the drawbridge's inner end close to the doors. Everyone, including the old Caliph, was down at the harbour watching the seamen take their craft away on what they hoped would be a crippling blow to their enemies in Israel.

He lost no time in passing into the depths of the rock-cut monastery, and quickly found that his suspicion that it was constructed very much on the same lines as the cliff-face abbeys of Palestine was quite correct. The masonry ran only to a point behind the chapel, from there on the abbey was a rabbit-warren of caves hewn out of the solid rock. Some of these were sited just inside the rock-face, and had square windows, very like the gunports that Jonathan had known when he was a cadet aboard H.M.S. *Conway* in the Menai Strait, which looked down on to the lights of the jetty.

As he looked through one of these windows Jonathan saw that complete darkness had fallen and was delighted to note that the ex-H.D.M.L. was already moving away from the quay, among a babel of voices which rose clearly in the still air of the land-locked little harbour. He felt the sweat running down his face in his anxiety, for everything now hung on whether the American had told the German that his passenger had missed the boat. If the German thought that Jonathan was with the H.D.M.L. and put to sea in ignorance of his having remained ashore, while the American also believed that, having missed his passage with him, the young journalist had joined the S-boat, then Jonathan had a clear twenty-four hours start with none of the pirates who still remained on the island even suspecting that he was ashore.

The few minutes that followed seemed to last an age as he sat on the sill waiting for any disturbance below which would show that the German had missed him. All remained normal enough, but Jonathan did not get his regular breathing fully restored until he saw the S-boat, outlined by several lights blazing on her decks to help her crew to stow away mooring-lines and make the final preparations for sea, gliding towards the harbour entrance, and, just before she passed through them, grow suddenly dark as every light on deck was extinguished.

Jonathan could scarcely believe in his good luck; he found it hard to credit that he was still on Skanthos without anyone knowing that he was there. If he could only make his preparations for a getaway without being seen, without anyone having an inkling that he was still ashore, he should be able to make that signal to the tanker and then escape in one of the half-dozen sailing-boats in the harbour. Everything depended on his lying completely hidden and unsuspected for the next twenty-four hours.

It was at the very moment when he was congratulating himself on his unexpected good fortune that a voice spat a challenge out of the darkness in the passage which lay beyond the cell in whose window he was sitting, clearly outlined against the flare of lights below him on the port.

" Who are you ? What are you doing in this secret place ? Answer or I'll fling this knife of mine through your ribs. Speak fast, or die ! "

Chapter 8

JONATHAN WARNS THE OIL-TANKER

The unknown quivered with deadly menace but, even as the man spoke Jonathan was aware that it was the voice of a very old man for its tones shook with age. Not that that made much difference to the accuracy with which the man might throw his knife. Obviously he must be skilled in its use or he would not have mentioned that he was holding a casting dagger instead of a pistol. All these considerations leaped through the lad's mind in a split second and, just as quick, was his reaction in throwing himself bodily from the sill and dropping to the dusty stone floor beneath the window.

The sharp tinkle of steel hitting stone came at once as a knife clattered against the edge of the sill, thrown low in the hope of transfixing the body of the target as he was falling. The deadly accuracy of the cast made Jonathan quake, but he felt silently along the floor and caught the knife which had fallen close behind him. It was a heavy weapon, its haft loaded to make it the more efficient for casting, and, as he drew it towards him, he felt its needle-point and the razor-sharpness of its edge. Certainly it was the weapon of a man who thought a great deal of his deadly art.

"Speak, thou Moslem swine!" the voice went on. "I have four more knives. Speak or die and know that the darkness makes no difference to Brother Alexius, whose blindness gives him the advantage over your eyes in these dark caverns where once holy men dwelt in prayer and mortification before devils in human shape drove them out. Speak or die, for I will throw another knife towards where I can hear your foul breathing. No man comes into these sacred galleries, for that was the agreement we made. The darkness is for Brother Alexius and the ghosts of his martyred brethren, the front of the holy house for you infidel dogs. My patience grows thin, so speak or perish!"

"I am no Moslem, Brother Alexius," Jonathan said in the same Arabic that the terrible old man in the darkness was using. "In the Name of the Father and of the Son and of the Holy Ghost I swear to you that I am a Christian and not of the Arab blood."

"What?" and the word was almost a shriek. "Have I almost shed Christian blood in my deep ignorance? May God and His Holy Mother forgive me for my sinful hastiness. I swear that I believed you to be an Infidel, and you cannot doubt that surely it is a sweet thing to slay the Unbeliever, or so our fathers thought when they came with the Red Cross on their surcoats to win back Jerusalem the Blessed."

This convinced the lad, as nothing else could have done, that he was dealing with a madman; with some poor lunatic who might have been one of the monks who had once lived in the peaceful sanctuary of Skanthos before the Nazis destroyed the community which had dwelt there for well over twelve centuries.

"Brother Alexius," Jonathan replied, keeping his voice steady, "I am a Christian who wishes to go to the Holy Land, but I was taken prisoner by the Moslems who now infest this island of yours. Will you not help me to get away? Listen, they plot to destroy a big ship which will pass south of here to-morrow night, and the only way in which we can save her is for me to use their signal-station to send out a warning of the awful thing they mean to do. Can you help me to save this ship and all the men who sail in her?"

"Are they Christians?" the old voice in the darkness asked with hoarse, cracked insistence.

"Of course," Jonathan assured him, hoping that the tanker's crew were not Lascars, Chinamen or any other type which might not meet with the mad old monk's approval. "Who else but Christians would sail in a ship flying the flag of a Christian country?"

Brother Alexius appeared to be quite convinced and shambled forward until he was alongside

Jonathan who, meanwhile, had risen rather gingerly from the dusty floor of the cave, not quite sure whether a length of steel would not slither in between his ribs. To be alone with a homicidal maniac, or with someone who appeared to be a close imitation of one, is not an enviable position and Jonathan felt his peril very keenly. There was no way out of it, however, so, putting the best possible face on things he stood up to humour the knife-throwing old gentleman.

Brother Alexius asked him his nationality and when Jonathan told him, the old monk started to speak in the English of a cultured man, but with the clipped precision of a student who has learned it mainly from books.

" Come with me," the old man said. " Hold my hand, for my blindness makes these dark tunnels and passages as clear to me as they would be in noonday light to you. Step out boldly, there is nothing to fear."

Jonathan did as he was bid although it cost a deal of resolution to step smartly along when he could not see a hand in front of his face once they had turned out of the cell with its glimmering square of dim light shining through the window. Brother Alexius, however, steadied him as he marched by placing a hand on his elbow and led the way with steps that never faltered. At long last Jonathan heard their footfalls echoing hollowly against a distant roof, instead of the patient padding which had lasted ever since they quitted the cell in the rock-face.

" We are crossing the Cathedral-vault," the old monk said quietly. " This was the choir of the monks who lived here in the days of persecution before the Emperor Constantine transferred the capital of the world from Rome to his new city on the Bosphorus. The old saints lie buried here, each little pile of holy bones in its own pigeon-hole in the south wall. You tread on holy ground, young Englishman."

Jonathan shuddered; he did not hold any strong views about ghosts but this felt as weird a place as any he could imagine. As his footfalls ceased to echo and his shoulder brushed against a stone wall he felt better to know that he was no longer in the ancient charnel-house.

" Only a little way further," Brother Alexius said, comfortingly, " before we reach the Great Shaft, where I have my little room."

" Here is my cell," the monk said after they had turned several corners. " You will find candles on the little altar which I light to do honour to the Blessed Lady when I recite the Office, although they are of no practical use to me. Flint and steel lie beside them in my tinder-box. You will find it if you feel along the wall. No, wait, better to let me do it, then nothing is liable to get upset by clumsy movements in the darkness. Stand still until I light the candles."

Flint and steel scraped together, causing a little shower of sparks before the tinder suddenly caught in a tiny burst of golden-flame. Brother Alexius, feeling the warmth of the fire, turned and with unerring exactness lit the wicks of two tall candles which, to Jonathan's infinite amazement were instantly reflected in a dazzling sparkle of blue, blood-red, green, flashing white and the soft sheen of pearls, hundreds of them all set in the glowing sheen of red gold.

It was an ikon, an almost life-size representation of the Blessed Virgin and Child, with every fold of the garments and curve of the features shown in low-relief on the shining gold that formed its base. But it was the crowns the two figures wore which reflected the candle flames in that glory of multi-coloured light ; rubies, emeralds, sapphires, pearls and diamonds of the finest water, and few of them smaller than a man's little finger-nail scintillated and glowed with the flickering of the yellow flames.

Brother Alexius laughed softly. " I hear your gasp of wonder, my son," he said shortly. " You should be on your knees in prayer for you are looking at a blessed sight that men have not seen for many generations. Your eyes are set on the wonder working Theotokos of Skanthos, Our Lady of the Islands, which men have worshipped ever since the days when my namesake, Alexius Comnenus, was Emperor in Constantinople. He gave it to our Abbey 900 years ago as a thank-

" Hurling himself straight at the Chinaman's knees in a flying rugger tackle he brought Chenghoo crashing to the ground."

offering for the salvation of the Imperial Court from the Frankish crusaders who swarmed down on him on their way to recover the Holy Land."

" It's wonderful and it's beautiful," Jonathan began, for he had never imagined such loveliness, nor dreamed of so great a display of priceless jewels. " It must be priceless."

" It is *holy*," the aged monk rebuked him, " and, consequently it is beyond any question of price. I have brought you here, believing in your Christianity, but you had best know that you can never find your way out of this labyrinth of passages without my aid. So, if you are a liar, and if your purpose is to slay me and hope to escape with our sacred treasure, you had best abandon all such thoughts. Many robbers have tried to penetrate this Web of Skanthos to steal it. You may still find the dried piles of their bones in the miles of corridors, at the places where they fell down and died lost in the labyrinth."

" I have not the least intention of robbing you, Brother," Jonathan protested, sounding very angry. The indignation in his fresh, young voice must have carried conviction to the old man, for he smiled and quietly laid aside the bundle of throwing knives that he had been carrying. The lad shivered a little as he realised what a fearsome enemy a blind but expert knife-thrower would be to anyone who might be trying to force his way through the maze of tunnels the monk had called the Web of Skanthos.

The monk produced food and a bottle of black Mavrodaphne wine from a recess in the rocky walls. He put the repast in front of his guest, but Jonathan scarcely touched it for he had had his evening meal with the pirates only a couple of hours earlier, and so did little more than to be courteous in accepting the hospitality offered to him. As he ate he told the old monk about the Red Cormorant and said how anxious he was to recover the ancient Scriptural manuscripts before they were lost for ever.

Brother Alexius listened intently and all the apparent craziness fell away from him as he listened to his guest's story.

" You have a stout and gallant heart, my son," he said, when Jonathan had finished. " My heart warms towards you for, knowing how great is your peril from these Moslem pirates, you are voluntarily risking your life in an effort to save that ship. Fear nothing, I will lead you to the door of the house that they use for their radio-signalling. I will also arrange that you shall have a boat to leave the island afterwards. Forgive my asking, but do you know how to send signals in this new business of radio ? "

" Sparks—I mean the radio-officer aboard my ship, was a great friend of mine, Reverend Brother," Jonathan replied. " I have always been interested in radio and he taught me how to use a transmitting-key. As I have no code-books I shall have to send the message in plain language so if the pirate-ships are listening they will know that they have been betrayed and will head back for Skanthos at their top speed."

"That must befall as God wills," Brother Alexius replied quietly. "Meanwhile we must do what we can. Go to sleep, my friend, I will take you to a chamber where you will be cool and comfortable and I will call you in the morning. Rest well, for there is much before you."

Jonathan would have preferred to discuss his plans but the old monk never wasted a word, and having said what he wanted would take no denial. Less than ten minutes later Jonathan was lying on a stone-shelf in an adjoining cell, with soft-textured Greek blankets making him a luxurious bed. To his own surprise he promptly fell asleep, never suspecting that his host had mixed a small dose of a harmless herbal sleeping-mixture in the glass of black wine which he had handed to him after he had climbed between the blankets.

When he awoke the room was bathed in a soft, greyish light and to his surprise he saw that a dim and diffused daylight was coming through a long, lancet-shaped window cut in the rock. The noise he made in stirring was very little but it was quite enough to bring the blind monk from his devotions in front of the bejewelled, golden ikon next door, bearing a plate of olives, bread and slices of a white and salty cheese, with a curiously carved but exquisite golden cup, which looked like a chalice. Jonathan protested against using so beautiful a thing as an ordinary cup, but Brother Alexius merely smiled and bade him not to worry.

"Gold is of no more use than pewter, my son," he said. "It is only the artificial value that man sets upon it which makes it valuable in our eyes. Drink, that was once the Emperor of Eastern Rome's own cup, but it will serve its turn as your tumbler."

The rest of that day was spent in those strangest of surroundings and Jonathan was a little stunned to learn that a vast treasure was hidden in the subterranean vaults. Skanthos, so the monk told him, had, centuries before, been one of the holiest shrines in the islands, but its more glorious days were over long before Constantinople fell to the Turks in 1453. It was believed that the abbey's treasures had been removed to help to buy help during the last defence of the Imperial City, but, as Brother Alexius explained, the abbot of those days had concealed them in the heart of the Web of Skanthos, where they had lain ever since, their presence known only to the Superior of the monastery and to the Prior, his second-in-command.

"I was Prior when the Germans came and slaughtered the brethren," Brother Alexius replied. "It was by sheer chance that I happened to be deep in the Web, repairing the filigree work of a ceremonial crown, and that saved me, for when I returned to the monastery all was silent with the silence of death. The abbot lay dead in his own chair and those of the twelve brethren, for we had become a tiny community compared to the hundreds of monks who once lived here, who had not been killed, were gone in the German boats along with all the survivors of our island population."

He went on to say he believed that Jonathan was the answer to years of prayers he had made to the Blessed Virgin and her Child, in which he had asked for an honest man to come to Skanthos, one who might be told of the secret of the treasure, so that if he, Brother Alexius, should die, they might never be lost. In all earnestness he begged Jonathan to swear on oath that, if anything went wrong, he would see that the treasures were returned to the Patriarch of Constantinople, the Head of his Church. Once Jonathan had taken the oath which the old monk administered at the altar, Brother Alexius took him entirely to his heart and showed him many things about the island.

He explained that the grey daylight came down what was called the Shaft, cut in the hill's heart and leading down from the craggy summit of Mount Skanthos, the crown of the island. The peak had never been climbed because its last fifty yards was a needle-shaped cone with slopes, so precipitous and bare that no one had ever succeeded in its escalade. The Shaft, cut in ancient days, was the reason why the air in the many miles of vaults and tunnels remained pure, for it drew the fresh currents through them towards the lofty summit.

"There is one exit, however," Brother Alexius told him, "through which I can lead you to a point very near to the topmost house of the village, the one where the radio-transmitter is. Its doorway is hidden in the ruins of an ancient chapel on the mountain-slopes, from which you should be able to approach the signal-station without being seen when the island is shrouded in darkness. Now you must rest again, for I have many things to which to attend, if you are to get away to-night. You will need a boat and that will need both time and toil. Rest and sleep, my son, and so garner fresh strength."

During the long hours of aching silence and utter loneliness that followed Jonathan cat-napped but he was often awake. The horror of the deep underground place in which he lay, the feeling of death and decay all round him got so badly on his nerves that he shouted with joy and relief when, long after the grey light in the Shaft had faded, Brother Alexius suddenly appeared, as abruptly as though he was a spirit taking physical shape in the candle-light. It was uncanny the fashion in which the old, stoop-shouldered, white-whiskered man in his rusty black cassock and stove-pipe, brimless hat, could move so utterly silently.

" All is ready, my son," he announced. "It is now fallen full dark in the outside world. Let us go. Follow me and hold my hand for we have far to travel."

After nearly an hour of walking in the black darkness, Brother Alexius suddenly halted and steadied Jonathan as he stumbled against him. As they stopped Jonathan became aware of a great swishing and rustling, mingled with the distant moaning of something that sounded like a great storm of wind and rain.

" The weather is unfortunate," the old monk said. " A savage *Shemali*, the bitter, black, north-wind, has sprung up and is howling through the islands. You can feel it here, for we are within a few feet of the exit on to the mountainside through the ancient ruins of the chapel. Is it essential that you should send the radio-message, my son, for I doubt if you can escape from Skanthos while this storm lasts ? "

" If I don't," Jonathan replied, through set teeth, for he was only too well aware of the danger that he would run once the signal was despatched, " the ship will be attacked by those piratical swine and all her crew will be lost. This storm will make little difference to them ; fatal though it may be to smaller boats. I must send it, Reverend

Brother, no matter what the consequences may be. It is eighty-odd lives against my own single one."

He felt embarrassed at speaking so theatrically, but knew that he must be very explicit if he was to convey his meaning to the blind man.

"Then go with God, my boy," the old man said. "May His Blessed Mother guard you through the dangers which lie before you. Now I know that I have done well in choosing you to learn our secret, for was it not said, nigh on two thousand years ago, that there is no love like that which lays down its life for a friend? Come."

Extremely glad that the old man had ceased talking in such a high-falutin way, for Jonathan felt acutely uncomfortable under such unusual talk, though he stepped cautiously forward under the monk's guiding hand. Once they were outside among the shattered walls of the ruined chapel the savage force of the Black Norther plucked at them as though it possessed steel fingers, while the whole dark mountainside seemed to be stirring and writhing as though it was a living thing perishing in agony.

"Over there, fifty yards away," Brother Alexius said, his lips brushing the lad's ear, pointing in the direction of the harbour. "Scramble down over that ledge and you will see the lights of the signal-station. They are screened from seawards but the pirates inside are not so particular about the windows which face the hill."

Jonathan wondered how the blind man knew that detail, but he passed no comment, for Brother Alexius had shown so many surprising qualities and attributes that nothing he did could astonish his comrade. He quickly found that the old monk had told the truth for, as he thrust his head over the ledge, there, not thirty yards away were the glowing windows of a house while, above the roar and scream of the rushing storm, he heard the whining hum of the generators and the coughing exhaust of their engines.

So far as he could tell from such a distance there were three men in the building, one of whom was busy near the engine in the back room, another was lounging against the wall smoking a cigarette, while, as Jonathan came closer and got his eye on the level of the sill, he saw a third man, wearing a green eye-shade, who was sitting on a swivel chair with a pencil in his hand and head-phones on his ears, apparently listening to a message that was coming through. All three would have to be settled before he could get to the transmitter to despatch his message, but without any other weapon than the dagger he had picked up from Brother Alexius's store, he did not see how he could overpower them.

The titanic wind whistled and roared around the house. Jonathan had to hang on for dear life as he reached the corner of the building to find a sheer drop yawning beneath him, for the terrace of rock on which the house stood fell abruptly away—its main approach from the village was by a long flight of stairs hewn in the solid mountainside leaving a precipice on either side. While he lay still, gasping for breath in that terrific hurly-burly of the gale, he heard someone cursing as he fought his way up the stairs, followed by a furious hammering on the door as the newcomer bawled for instant admittance.

A shaft of light stabbed the night to seawards for a moment as the door was thrown open and then the front of the house became dark again as it was slammed behind the newly-admitted visitor. Jonathan crept back to the rear window and saw that the operator had dropped his headphones and laid down his pencil; he had swivelled round in his chair and was talking to a man clad in streaming yellow oilskins who was gesticulating furiously, while the remaining two were already reaching for their own waterproof clothing hanging on the hooks at one side of the door.

Some sudden emergency must have arisen in the port, possibly a boat had broken adrift in the surge setting in from the open sea, Jonathan never learned that detail. Whatever it was the new arrival was demanding help and the other two men of the radio-crew evidently thought it was necessary for them to leave the comparative comfort of their station and accompany him. Jonathan lay very still and watched them go out, scarcely daring to believe that such a fortunate coincidence could have occurred so opportunely but determined to take the fullest advantage of it.

The three men left and Jonathan grinned as he heard the rumble of their cursing as they dashed through the door and out into the storm. Then he became grimly silent, waiting only long enough for them to be well out of earshot before making his own entry into the house. He soon saw that it would be almost impossible to get inside without giving the operator at the table a chance to press some alarm-bell, to draw a gun or to make an outcry. Boldness and sheer impudence promised the best results and, creeping round the house, bracing himself against the roar and tug of the storm while he moved along the foot-wide cement ledge over the sheer drop, he reached the landing at the head of the stairs, where he knocked loudly on the front door. It opened almost at once and revealed in the bright light of the gap stood the figure of the radio-operator.

The man had no intention of being taken by surprise. Firmly grasped in his right hand and held level with his waist, was the blued-steel shape of an automatic-pistol, and, as quick as a flash the man, seeing an unknown face in front of him, tried to slam the door in Jonathan's face and, as he did so, the lad saw the operator's knuckles grow white as he tightened his finger on his trigger.

CHAPTER 9

THE BLACK NORTHER

JONATHAN'S fist travelled upwards with the speed of a piston-rod, connecting sweetly with the unshaven chin of the man trying to slam the door. There was not a split-second between the English lad's living or dying for the crooked trigger-finger had almost completed its pull when that whizzing uppercut found the point of the man's jaw and spread temporary blackness through his villainous brain. Jonathan waited for no more—that door of glowing light must not be permitted to shine forth into the storm-filled night for one single second longer than was absolutely necessary, for fear that someone down below might return to see what had happened to make the operator open it.

Kicking the dropped pistol into the room, he bent down, grabbed the operator by the shoulders and dragged him within, slamming the door shut behind him with a wag of his buttocks, without even taking his hands off the fallen man. Jonathan pocketed the pistol, patted the radio operator all over to make sure that he was carrying no other weapons and turned to look for a bit of rope with which to bind him. That momentary inattention almost cost the lad his life, for he had no sooner turned away than the man was on his feet, and grabbing a heavy spanner he found ready to his hand, sprang murderously to the attack.

Jonathan's years in the barracks of the Palestine Police and in the ships of the Red Diamond Line had not been wasted—he knew very well how to take care of himself in a free-for-all, while in the *Conway* he had been the heavyweight champion of the grand old training-ship. Stepping lithely to one side he delivered his own speciality, a left-hook and right-uppercut to the jaw, followed by a swift sinking of a straight left into the man's body close to the solar-plexus, with the result that the sallow-faced fellow, who looked as if he might be one of those Spanish refugees who are fairly common in the Isles of Greece, dropped as though he had been poleaxed.

Long before he had the least chance to recover the unfortunate radio-operator was lashed securely, hands together and with each wrist bound to his ankles, which in their turn were drawn up behind him into the small of his back, while a large piece of adhesive-tape from a roll of the sticky stuff lying on the desk, served as a most excellent gag and yet allowed the captive to breathe through his nostrils. After dragging him into a large cupboard at one side of a room which looked as though it might have been built for a kitchen, Jonathan fairly threw himself at the transmitter. A quick glance showed him that it was the usual type fitted in British merchantmen, and very similar to the one aboard *Symondsbury Mote*, so that a few seconds were enough to bring the transmitter into action.

With the key in his hands and his ears covered with the headphones Jonathan hammered away in the Morse Code, straining his ears for an acknowledgement. For long minutes none came, but, desperately afraid that he might be interrupted before he could warn the tanker, he kept his fingers and hand working rhythmically over the heavy transmitting-key.

" *Moslem pirates will attempt torpedo oil tanker approaching Haifa from Venezuela to-night. Pirate craft are one old German S-boat, one ex-British H.D.M.L. S-boat carries torpedoes. H.D.M.L. armed guns only. Both boats informed tanker's course and position. Unless tanker takes wide evasive action she will be sunk to-night.*"

Throwing down the key Jonathan made for the back door, knowing that he could do no more. He had not heard anyone approaching, so that it was a shattering surprise when, as he pulled the back-door open after unbolting it, the front one crashed wide and the almighty gale roared devastatingly through the house, but not loud enough to drown the thunder of three pistol shots. Plaster sprang in gouts from the wall in front of him as he leaped through the door, where the bullets had hit within a foot of his head.

Out into the wild night he heard the angry whine of the rest of the man's magazine as he pulled the trigger and sent his remaining bullets into the darkness. Turning sharply to the left Jonathan scrambled up the cliff, and then, remembering his own pistol, pulled it out of the pocket into which he had crammed it, and as the man's body came into the lighted frame of the back-door, he fired three shots, and felt a savage joy as he watched the man sag to his knees. Five seconds later Brother Alexius's voice came out of the ruins bidding him jump quickly into cover.

As they hurried into the bowels of the mountain-side Jonathan told the old monk what he had done, and said how fervently he hoped that his radio-signal had been picked up and relayed to the threatened oil-tanker. But, to the old man's suggestion that he should take cover in the Web of Skanthos, Jonathan refused to listen.

"If they check up and find that no boat has left the island they will know that I am still here," he said firmly. "That will mean that they will strain every nerve to find me, and so find your refuge, find your treasure and commit sacrilege on the Holy Ikon. No, Brother Alexius, no matter how bad it may be out there, I've just got to go."

In actual fact Jonathan was not nearly so anxious about the Ikon as he was to get away from the island before all escape from Skanthos was cut off, but he knew that his argument of the Theotokos of Skanthos being in danger, was the most powerful one he could use to persuade the aged monk to lead him to the boat he had made ready. So it proved, for the threat to his shrine brought Brother Alexius into instant agreement, for he honestly believed that no mere human fears, nor even the terror-of-death should be allowed to bring his blessed relics into peril of being despoiled.

Without further argument he told Jonathan to keep hold of his hand and led him along many furlongs of steeply sloping tunnels until they halted, with the thundering boom and surge of the sea throbbing the air which was damp with the spray flung up by the huge waves breaking a few feet beneath them.

"We are at the foot of the cliffs outside the harbour," Brother Alexius explained. "This is a secret exit which was cut centuries ago to be used if infidels held the harbour and it became necessary for the brethren to escape. Our boat is kept here for it was one of our rules to keep this escape-port always ready, and since our brothers were taken away I have done my best to retain all the old things so far as I can. I have been working on the boat while you were resting. Her sails and gear are sound, there is fresh water aboard, and I have put some food in the lockers, but I fear that she won't live long in that smother of surf outside the Guardian Reef."

When Jonathan asked him what the Guardian Reef might be the old monk replied that it was a natural breakwater lying about fifty yards out with the seas smashing on its spouting rocks. He listened intently to the old man's description of the local sea and shore conditions and then said that it was high time he was away. They stepped the mast, with its single lateen sail, after Jonathan had close-reefed the canvas. The rudder was then shipped and Jonathan took his place in the stern-sheets at Brother Alexius's command. The launching trough cut in the rock was not unlike that of some lifeboat stations on the British coast, sloping steeply down to the water surging up the cave-mouth.

"Shout when you are ready, my English friend," the old monk cried. "I will pull the bolt as soon as you do and that will launch you. May God guard you."

"God bless you, too, holy Brother," Jonathan cried, making his voice rise above the confusion of the elements. "I'll see that your monastery is saved if I live. Thank you and now—Let her go!"

A thin hammering rose above the roar of the sea for a couple of seconds and then, as though launched from a bow, the heavy, eighteen-foot swooped down the inclined slipway and with a mighty splash hit the water outside. Jonathan saw the gap in the wall of white surf leaping into the night and hauling in his sheet, laid the boat over on her side under the savage thrust of the wind. Without losing the way gained by her forceful launching, she jumped away like a race-horse. The seas were running criss-cross and wild inside the reef, but Jonathan's luck held good for a squall slammed his sail full. Almost before he knew what was happening, the boat had run out of the swirling danger at the foot of the cliffs and was swooping over the huge greybeards racing past the lee of Skanthos, whose crown towered against the storm-wrack.

Those first fury-filled minutes were the worst as he was tossed and thrown in all directions by the confused seas recoiling from the island's feet. He had to fight for every inch he won in his scramble to get away from the sharp-fanged rocks over which the mighty surges burst in a smothering cloud of roaring spray and spindthrift. Inch by inch he edged clear until, suddenly, the boat shot out of the lee of the island and the great gale was coming solidly at him with nothing to break its frenzy.

Fortunately it was blowing from the north which meant that, so long as he could keep from being capsized or pooped by one of the over-running water-hills piling up astern, every second was hurling him towards the coast of Palestine.

Jonathan had a very vivid mental picture of the chart—somewhere to port, over to the south-east, lay the vast mass of Cyprus which he hoped to pass well to westward, for he was almost sure that in such a gale the two pirate craft would be making their way home between the big British-owned island and the coastline of Syria.

His first fear was quickly succeeded by the exhilaration of finding himself able to cope with such a smother of wind and sea. But the ever-present peril never allowed a moment of inattention or carelessness—the smallest lapse on his part or a momentary hesitation at the tiller, and he would be hurled, spinning end over end, a shattered, dismasted wreck, to suffer a smothering death in the trough of the mighty seas.

On and on and on he sped, lifted by the onrush of one mighty sea-mountain, a brief pause on its crest as the boat was hurled forwards like a javelin in Neptune's quivering hand before it dipped, stern-up, bows low as it slipped down its reverse face, the next great wave poised over his transom as though it was about to smash this puny floating object which dared to defy its overweening majesty. Another pause while toppling destruction seemed certain, that nothing could save the thin planking and thinner canvas, ineffectual cordage and a mere human from being caught in a titanic hammer-blow by the toppling crest piling up, white-crested above and behind her, and then up would go the bows and the process started all over again.

Jonathan lost all sense of time—he was not even conscious of being weary, although every muscle and sinew was aching and searing with pain. The supreme joy of battle, that queer, very human triumph over all thoughts of personal destruction, had gripped him just as it had held his Viking forefathers in similar situations. In his great battle with the night-shrouded, tempest-bewildered sea nothing mattered save the fight itself, and the sheer joy of combat and the knowledge that only his own skill, his strength of purpose and the favour of God, could bring him through to life.

Dawn came with almost unbelievable swiftness, Jonathan could scarcely believe that the hours of darkness had passed so quickly, but there was no mistaking that the sky to eastward was growing paler. Then, to his utmost astonishment, he saw the shape of distant mountains away on his port quarter black against the first golden lances of the returning sun. He was astonished for he had run throughout the night at double the speed he had calculated to get so far that the crests of the Cypriot mountains should already lie astern. Another glance at the small compass, an old-fashioned brass-bound affair which dated at least from the 1840's, when Ibrahim Ali Pasha of Egypt was threatening the Sultan of Turkey.

He was running almost due south, and knew that he must try to make more easting if he was not to land somewhere on the Sinai Peninsula, or even the Nile Delta, both of which would be fatal so far as his attempt to find the Red Cormorant's message was concerned.

To haul the boat's head round to the south-eastward in front of that mighty gale was a perilous business, and it is probable that a more experienced seafarer than the youngster would never have tried it. Fortune favours the bold, one old adage says, but it is far more likely that it was " the cherub who sits up aloft and looks after the life of poor Jack " who saw Jonathan through that day of mountainous seas and black squalls which came hurtling down from the northward. The first exhilaration of combat died away as his bodily exhaustion increased. It was extremely hard physical toil to stay at that bucking tiller, humouring the reeling boat as she tried to come up into the wind forced by the drag of the leading edge of her single sail stepped so far forward in her eyes.

Some chunks of Brother Alexius's bread and hard, white, sheep's milk cheese, and a draught of water put fresh life into him as the boat plunged towards the distant coast of the Holy land far away beneath the sea-rim. Looking aft, judging the angle between his fore-and-aft line and the wake he was leaving behind him, Jonathan did his best to calculate his leeway, that is the amount the craft was being set sideways by the pressure of the wind on her quarter as she sped ahead. As a consequence of these calculations he eased her off a little more to the southward and hoped fervently that he would finally arrive in Palestine somewhere south of Haifa, for he could make no nearer guess at his landfall.

When the sun sank that evening beneath the black storm-wrack to starboard there was nothing in sight but the foam-capped waves charging down from windward in roaring majesty before retreating to leeward in hissing disappointment. Jonathan was almost flung overboard by the crazy, leaping motion of the craft when he stood upright as she soared on the crest of an especially huge wave, hoping to see whether the heights of the Carmel Range or the peaks of the Samaritan Mountains were in sight. But, when the darkness settled in storm-riven amid scurrying rags of cloud, there was still no sign of the Palestine Hills. Jonathan crouched down in the stern-sheets, fighting his insane but all-pervading desire to sleep and, for a while, thought of heaving-to. That evolution would have been quite impossible in so small a craft, he would have been swamped and over-run long before he could have got her round, while, to keep her pointing into the storm would have cost him as much in vigilance and close attention as running before it had done.

He knew that well enough of course, but the

planning of such a manoeuvre made at least a fine diversion for his thoughts from the roaring misery all round him. If the monks of Skanthos had only thought of putting a sea-anchor among her stores he would certainly have streamed it and so got some rest while the boat rode to it. But, as their imaginations had not reached that far, there was nothing he could do but keep his boat running before the gale and hope that he would not strike the shores of the Holy Land before dawn gave him a chance to see it in time.

He was wondering, too, whether his despairing signal to the oil-tanker had saved her. Had she turned away, or were her eighty-odd seamen lying dead in their sunken ship? Perhaps the storm might have proved their salvation by preventing the pirate-craft from pressing home their attacks? Jonathan hoped so with all his heart, but he was too tired to worry overmuch, and he might easily have sunk into a sleep which would certainly have been his last if, at that very moment when his brain was losing control of his limbs, the crashing thunder of heavy surf had not broken through the mental fog closing in on him.

He staggered upright, astonishment and fear filling his soul, and suddenly saw that the black mass dead ahead, stretching away on either bow, was not storm-wrack as he had believed it to be, but was the mass of the Palestinian hills which were filling the lower parts of the sky in those directions. Almost under the boat's forefoot a great gout of white foam suddenly exploded, while close by, less than a hundred yards at the port beam a huge wave smashed itself to a pale smother on a little headland and tore streaming across the spouting rocks.

Ahead, astern, on the beam, the white surf piled itself towards the clouds, the boat was so deeply entangled in the maze of reefs that there was no way out. As though the Sea knew what was happening and was triumphantly delivering the killing-stroke, a great black squall came shrieking in to end the existence of this puny floating thing which had for too long defied its dignity and outraged its majesty.

Up and ever up, soared the bows of the little boat, the stern sank, while, simultaneously, the tearing twisting motion as the long seas breaking on the shoaling sand and glancing off in all directions began to tighten their grip and pull at her keel. Up and over it went, its timbers creaking and cracking, the surf smashing harder, the almighty overwhelming rush of the cheated sea driving ever more strongly at his stern. With a sudden but utter collapse, the boat fell to pieces, smashed to splintered planks as with a final and terrible hammer-blow she struck the unforgiving sand, and the surf boiled white across her disintegration.

All was noise, confusion, blackness, roaring of

waters and the whirling scream and hiss of irresistible surf. Jonathan's last conscious thought as the sea threw him forward like a chip of driftwood was that this was the end of his adventuring and that the Red Cormorant's Hoard would never be found by Colonel Samway's son, who was now returning to the land of his birth, flung there, a speck of worthless flotsam, to perish on its storm-harried coastline.

Chapter 10

TRAPPED ON MOUNT CARMEL

Long past all ability to help himself, expecting death at any moment and not greatly worried at the prospect, Jonathan was carried shorewards on the crest of a great spindrift-crowned roller, soaring the blackness of the roaring night, as swiftly as though he had been deliberately surf-riding. By an almost miraculous chance his inert body was caught by a caprice of the sea a second before the huge roller broke and was thrown straight at one of the few patches of sand that were not littered by blocks of masonry torn from the crumbling walls of once-mighty Castle Pilgrim.

He was brought to his senses by the agonising pain that shot through him as he hit the sand and, even before the giant wave sent him spinning up the foaming beach among its racing spume, he was fighting for his life. His rolling, slithering speed slowed as the force of the wave began to fade before it started to recede seawards and even as he drove toes and fingers into the firm sand, Jonathan knew where he was, for Athlit, the modern name of the old castle of the Knights

Templar, is one of the favourite bathing-beaches used by Haifa business-men and officials.

The undertow dragged and tore at him, as though it was some great sea-monster anxious to suck this feeble human being back to play with it for a little longer before finally smashing it. Jonathan's fingers slipped through the sand, his toes dug a deepening water-filled furrow as he lay pressing his whole body as close to it as he could, while the white water hissed and bubbled and dragged and sucked sibilantly at every square inch of his body. Then, at the very second when the strain on his hands and muscles became intolerable, when he felt that he was being drawn back into the raging mass of storm-ridden darkness roaring behind him, the awful drag ended, and, knowing that he could endure no more of this savage tug-of-war, he staggered to his feet and lurched into a stumbling run to reach the higher part of the beach. Before he had covered many feet the next rushing wall of surf was screaming and hissing at his heels as though it was a monster afraid that its lawful prey was going to escape. It caught his knees, rose to his thighs in snarling rage and felled him before he could win clear, but he reached safety for the broken water rose no higher than his waist as he fell, at the moment when it started to recede to the deeps.

The recession saved him, for as he fell he was twisted broadside-on to the full fury of the breakers and if its strength had not already reached the top of its run, he would have been sucked back into the maw of the great fury so close behind him. He had to fight desperately, literally with teeth and all twenty nails, to save himself from death. He was so high up the beach that the water ran back very quickly and so gave him time to get on to his feet again and to lurch drunkenly along until he felt beneath his feet some sand where the surf did not reach, and then, unable to go an inch further, he collapsed in a pitiful heap, to all appearances a heap of wreckage that the sea had cast up in savage derision.

There is no tide, or, rather only a few inches of it on these shores, so that the edge of the sea came no closer while Jonathan lay on the sand, scarcely daring to believe that he was alive. He was gasping for breath and aching as though every bone in his body was broken and every sinew and muscle pulled and strained. He lay close on half-an-hour before he was able to summon sufficient strength, and nerve, to move off the beach and find a hiding-place. If, as he was now sure, he was at Athlit, he would not only be very close to an agricultural colony and salt-works established long before the ending of the British Mandate, but also to a big Transit camp for immigrants. The camp had once been a prison and lay just beyond the low foothills which cut off the saltpans and the ruins of the fortress of Castle Pilgrim from the plain that runs back to the bases of Mount Carmel, three or four miles to the eastward.

There would be Israeli soldiers at the camp, both to control the newcomers gathered there to await work and accommodation, and to act as reinforcements for the blockhouses of the Pass of El Keimun, which runs between the landward end of Mount Carmel and the Hills of Samaria, and gives access from the seaward to the Plain of Armageddon. The Samaritan hills are Arab territory so that Athlit is very close to the debatable frontier between Israeli and Moslem; twenty-five miles or so to the south-eastward lay Kuryet Jett, the village where the Red Cormorant had hidden the directions to find his Hoard. Jonathan forced himself along the beach knowing that he must be under cover before dawn if he did not wish to be arrested by the Israeli forces and probably shot as a spy by soldiers who were accustomed to taking swift action.

At first he thought that the castle-ruins seemed to be his best hiding-place but reflection showed that the old chambers around the Banqueting Hall and the caves within the shattered walls were too well known to be safe. The last thing anyone would expect, however, was that a fugitive should walk straight towards them! Why not go to the Transit-camp beyond the foothills and lose himself among the hundreds of immigrants newly arrived from Europe, who were waiting for jobs and accommodation? His clothing, once it was dry, was very similar to theirs and the fact that he spoke Hebrew fluently might carry him through the worst of his immediate dangers.

He found that it was sheer torture to walk at all, for he was extensively bruised by his buffeting and was almost blind with exhaustion. His long watchfulness in keeping the little boat running before the storm was beginning to overpower him, but, by summoning every last ounce of his reserve of strength, he managed to keep moving. His muscles limbered up as he used them so that soon he was making a fairly good speed towards the gap in the foothills where the ruins of the Templar Knights' watch-tower guards the shallow pass running towards the fortress. The gaping pits of the quarries whence the stone for Haifa Harbour was taken in 1930, gave him ample cover up to the rear of the hutted camp beside the road. As he drew nearer he was glad to see that the barbed-wire which, in British times, had prevented the escape of the illegal immigrants imprisoned there, had been taken away so that it was now more like a village than a jail.

Voices over to his left warned him, as he drew closer to the huts that there were soldiers on guard, watching for bands of Arab irregulars who in some sudden foray from the hills might try to raid the camp. Jonathan promptly went to ground feeling so utterly spent that he could no longer travel and still maintain extreme caution. Once he was down, lying in a little pocket among the rocks at the edge of the great quarry, he found that it was quite impossible for him to rise again. He desperately resisted the rising tide of sleep but the fight was beyond his powers and, almost before he knew it deep, black and merciful unconsciousness wafted smoothly over him. Jonathan sank into a slumber from which the discharge of a field-gun in the immediate neighbourhood would not have wakened him.

He awoke to find he was lying in deep shadow although the countryside, beyond the crack between the boulders which flanked his hiding-place was bathed in strong sunlight. He lay without moving for some time, while memory slowly returned to give him realisation of where he was and his chances of survival. After a while he rose to his feet, feeling wretchedly weak and ill, his thirst tearing at his throat, and a fierce craving for substantial food. That was not surprising for he had not eaten anything but a few morsels of stale bread and cheese for nearly four days and starvation was making him light-headed.

With a start he realised that he must have slept for about twelve hours, for the sun was far down in the west, with the tip of the shattered Keep of Athlit castle showing over the top of the intervening ridge. Not more than three hundred yards away the brown, creosoted huts of the Transit

Camp stood etched sharply against the palm-trees of the old Aaronsohn Experimental Farm, which has lain neglected for years, and the glory of the sunset on the sea. The gale had died down and the evening was fine and warm so that hundreds of men and women had come out of the lines of hutments and were either sitting on the crest of the low foothills, or swimming in the gently creaming surf fifty feet beneath them. While Jonathan watched he saw the train from Haifa come down the railway line which lay between him and the beach, and he saw people in the coaches waving to new-arrivals from Europe and Morocco who were sitting on the rocks and waving back.

An efficient-looking Israeli armoured-car came out of the camp and passed slowly up the road towards the entrance to the Keimun Pass, while a knot of soldiers marched back from the sea's edge with their towels knotted round their sunburned throats. They passed out of Jonathan's sight behind the lines of brown huts where, a few minutes later, a bugle blew for the evening muster and the guard-mounting. On a tall staff in the middle of the camp, and also from the battlements on the top of the Crusader watch-tower, flew the blue and white ensign of Israel with its Shield of David emblazoned upon it.

One party of young men, about twenty strong, were less than a hundred yards from where Jonathan was lying, and as they rose to their feet

"He delivered the injured Sheikh into the capable hands of the Moslem doctor."

and turned to make their way back towards the camp, he also rose to his feet, and fighting his inclination to stagger with sheer weakness, walked along behind them as soon as they had passed his hiding-place. No one paid him any attention but, even if they had done so their eyes would have been quickly diverted by cheering and shouting rising from the direction of the railway-station, where a fresh batch of new immigrants from the misery of Displaced Persons' camps in Europe were detraining after being landed in Haifa.

Hearing the excited shouts as people hurried down to see whether long-lost friends or relations might be among the newcomers, Jonathan mingled with the throng and was soon engulfed in their excited ranks. A knot of blue-clad Israeli police, whose uniforms bore a strong resemblance to those of the British Force of a few years earlier, quietly marshalled the column of fresh arrivals which, with Jonathan in their midst, swung singing along the dusty road to the Camp reception office.

The upshot of it all was that, despite his fatigue, and probably because no one expected any trickery, Jonathan won his way into the camp, where he was allotted a bed and an identity-card which entitled him to draw rations in the mess-shed and also what clothing he needed to make himself presentable. Both physically and mentally Jonathan was almost beyond caring what happened to him by this time, but by keeping the thought of his resolution and his mission well in mind, he forced himself to go through the formalities of reception without rousing any suspicion, had a good and sustaining meal, and then fell on to the bed in the long hut to which he had been assigned, and was soon fast asleep.

By the time he was roused next morning by the rest of his hut-mates hurrying out to wash and to get their breakfast, he was almost back to his normal self. The long rest had set him up afresh and, after he had eaten a meal of fish, olives, rice and bread, he felt a new man and ready for anything that might come his way.

Few of his neighbours spoke any Hebrew, for that is a language learned, usually, only after the immigrants have been some time in Palestine, and he was very careful not to make himself conspicuous by any foolish display of his own knowledge of the tongue. But, as the day wore on, he quietly weighed up his chances of slipping away, but was growing more and more disturbed and anxious as he saw how tight was the guard set upon the frontiers of the State of Israel. That frontier lay less than four miles away on the slopes of the grey hills rising above the inland edges of the Plain of Sharon, on whose northern limits the camp is sited, but he already saw that, as an ordinary civilian he had small chance of approaching it, let alone of getting across.

Kuriyet Jett, the village he was aiming to reach, lies further south among those foothills, and his main problem was to decide the best route by which he might reach it. If he worked south, moving in Israeli territory, the settlements grew more numerous and thicker the nearer he came to Tel Aviv, while, if he wriggled through the Arab lines and reached the hills he would find very little cover on their stony flanks. In his Jewish pioneer's clothing he would make a conspicuous target for any Arab irregular rifleman lurking among the boulders and scrub. As there seemed to be no immediate answer he decided to let matters rest for a day or two, at least a rest would allow him fully to recover his strength and to study the situation. But he dared not wait too long for there was no saying what Cheng-Loo's gang might not be doing in the meanwhile ; Jonathan reminded himself that he was already a long time behind the schedule which his father had laid down for him, and consequently their gang might already have discovered the hoax which had been played on them by the burglary which diverted them to Saudi Arabia.

The days passed quickly and by pretending to be an American-Jew who wished to become an Israeli citizen, and by doing his best to imitate a Brooklyn accent, Jonathan found himself being accepted by his hut-mates as an ordinary youngster filled with enthusiasm as most of the others were but possessing no special interest. The camp was a fairly happy place; there was nothing of the prison about it for people were free to come and go, and beyond their anxieties as to where they might be sent, and what work would be found for them, the newcomers to the Holy Land seemed content. There was plenty to do for all the younger men, and a great many of the girls, were given military training from seasoned veterans of the Haganah, who told them stirring tales of the fighting against the regular Arab armies during the first months of the new State's existence.

On his fifth morning a sergeant came round the huts asking for volunteers to work on a new road that the army was driving through the Keimun Pass towards the settlements on the Plain of Armageddon which lies beyond the mountain-wall blocking the eastern horizon. Jonathan was one of the first to step forward as he hoped that this duty might give him the chance of slipping away and reaching the Arab lines to make his way to Kuryet Jett.

The working-party was taken to the scene of their labours in half-a-dozen lorries escorted by an armoured-car at both the head and the tail of the convoy with their guns trained on the slopes of the Samaritan Hills. They crossed the main Haifa-Tel Aviv road in the middle of an olive grove covering the intersection of the laneway to Athlit which had the burned out hulk of a British police-station at the junction to show the intensity of the fighting that had once raged in these now apparently peaceful surroundings.

But that the countryside was not in the least peaceful became fully apparent as soon as they entered the Pass, for Arab strong-points and khaki-clad patrols of the Iraqi army on the right-hand slopes, faced Israeli positions on the flanks of Mount Carmel to the left, while the road was evidently being treated as the actual border and also as a neutral-ground by both sides. Jonathan, who was sitting facing outboard in his lorry, with a rifle and a cotton bandolier of cartridges lying on the floor out of sight at his feet, ready to be brought into action should they be needed, felt all the thrill and adventure of this debatable borderland between two races, two cultures, two Faiths and two widely differing ways of life; between the Crescent and the foes whom it had hated and scorned for centuries, and now to its angry astonishment it found strong enough to resist its might.

The lorries lurched on travelling more and more slowly as the surface became rougher until they reached the place where they were to work on this vital stretch of strategic roadway, and, unloading picks and shovels, the men started to work. The armoured cars remained at action-stations ready to repel any attack by fanatical Arab irregulars who might defy the armistice and try to strike a blow at the hated infidels. Jonathan sweated mightily as he toiled with his pick at the side of the road, one of a gang who were cutting a drainage-ditch. The summer sun, beating on the dry, arid ground and the grey rocks, blasted the valley between the mountains with a heat that felt as solid as a thick blanket.

Noonday brought the workmen a short rest as they sat in whatever shade they could find and ate the cold meats and bread brought on the lorries. While they did so a patrol of Arab soldiers, wearing the uniforms of the Iraqi Army came down the slopes and stood among them. The Israel soldiers from the armoured-cars, tough, seasoned fighting men of the Haganah jested with the Arabs, but the newcomers from Europe maintained a sulky silence, and even murmured angrily against men of their own race fraternising with the hated Moslems. Jonathan, however, was listening very intently to the conversation of the soldiers, and began to build a general picture for himself of what was going on behind the Arab lines. It was here that he committed a mistake which might very easily have been fatal, for he carelessly showed so keen an interest in what was being said that a few of his fellow-labourers noted it and grew suspicious. One of the first things that was impressed on all new arrivals was the paramount need for Public Security ; they had been told that spies of all nations were rife in Israel, traitors who were seeking information for the Arabs or for people in the outside world who detested the new State.

None of his mates, lounging beneath the sparse shelter of the olive-trees, said anything, and so Jonathan had no idea that he was an object of their suspicion when, after the end of the noonday break, their work on the road was resumed. The Arab troops quietly drifted away, but, towards sunset others arrived who were anxious to trade bottles of olive-oil against sweets, soap and articles of clothing. Jonathan was treated to an exhibition of the strange state of affairs along this most debatable frontier in the world, where bitter shortages of some of the most ordinary things of living exist on both sides.

By the time work was ending for the day he had made up his mind not to return to the Transit-Camp. He intended to hide among the rocks until the lorries had gone, and then, by waiting for full darkness, to get through the laxly-held Arab lines, while at the same time carefully avoiding the vigilance of the Israeli troops on the slopes of Carmel behind and above him. He had not the least reason to suspect that half-a-dozen of his mates were watching him very keenly, expecting him to do something that would prove him to be the spy that they suspected he was. They did not betray their knowledge that he had failed to join them while the lorries were loading the crews, but waited until the very last moment before calling the sergeant in charge of the escort.

Jonathan meanwhile had hidden himself behind a large boulder between two olive-trees a hundred yards on the Carmel side of the road, hoping that the convoy would move off quickly and so end his anxiety. But when it failed to start and he heard excited voices, he peered out and saw that most of the men in the lorry in which he should have been seated, were talking angrily to the soldiers and pointing straight at his hiding-place, he knew that he had not been so clever as he had thought. The sun-burned sergeant turned his light-grey, fighting-man's eyes straight towards Jonathan's hiding-place while, in a general chorus, the labourers in the lorry shouted the Hebrew word for " Spy ! " and yelled to the soldiers to dig out the lurking traitor.

Feeling as helpless as a rabbit facing a stoat, Jonathan watched the sergeant motion to two of his men to advance and examine the space behind the boulders, before he turned to hush the excited clamour of the labourers in the lorry. With their rifles held at the ready the two hardy-looking young Haganah troopers came swiftly up the slope, their grim faces plainly showing that they intended to stand no nonsense. There was no possible way of escape—if he tried to run he would be shot down long before he could reach substantial cover. If he stayed where he was and waited to be dragged out of his hiding-place, his end would be just as quick and certain. Neither the soldiers nor the labourers were in the least likely to show any mercy to a man whom they had caught trying to desert to the Arabs with precious information, as they would be convinced he was doing.

Utterly helpless, Jonathan lay quite still, and desperately made up his mind to put as good a face on things as he could. With quiet determination he prepared to show no cowardice if a sudden and violent death was to come to him within the next few seconds.

Chapter 11

THE CAVE CALLED THE SORCERER'S WORKSHOP

The Arab bandits sprang their ambush with such sudden and overwhelming ferocity, and so total a lack of warning that the men in the lorries had small chance to save themselves. The bullet-storm sleeting from the rough hill-slopes was so accurate and so devastating that the immigrant labourers and the khaki-clad Haganah soldiers dropped before its withering blast without much chance to hit back. The two soldiers who were stalking towards the boulder behind which Jonathan was crouching, dropped dead among the first casualties.

Those two men probably formed the reason for the shots being fired at that particular moment; the ambushers, ensconced in their deep cover, may have believed that the pair of soldiers were quietly making their way to some rifle-pit from which they could command the lurking marksmen's positions. But whatever the reason may have been the narrow valley rocked with the din of musketry and the deeper crash of bombs bursting on the road. The angry taunting shouts of the labourers in the lorries egging the two soldiers on to find the traitor were instantly changed to screams of fear and agony in the few seconds before their cries were silenced in death by the whining bullets.

It was several minutes before the clatter of machine-guns came from the armoured-cars and from high on the Carmel slopes, followed by the disciplined shooting of the Arab regulars, who were as anxious as their Israeli opposite numbers to punish this flagrant breach of the truce perpetrated by the irresponsible fanatics who are insistent in their refusal to keep any peace with the new-comers of the young State of Israel. In the confusion Jonathan saw his chance and, as the darkness gathered, he slipped swiftly from one rock to the next, hoping that neither Arab nor Jew would open fire at his flitting figure.

He was very fortunate for he got safely away from the immediate neighbourhood of the ambush and had reached the truncated cone of Tel Keimun, the site of a long lost Biblical city, when he stumbled right into one of the positions in which the attackers during the day had mustered secretly. Among other stores he found several sets of Arab clothing, an *abiya* mantle of camel's wool which had probably been left behind by its owner who did not wish to be hampered by it in the murderous affray he was setting out to join. There were also several *keffyehs*, head-cloths, together with the *egals*, the twin head-ropes which hold these cloths to the wearers' brows. The Arabs, as usual, had fought in their *tekiyeh* skull-caps, afraid that the flowing headcloths might be noted too easily while they were taking up their positions prior to launching their onslaught on the Jews beneath.

Jonathan dressed himself in the disguise of a young Arab, and, throwing the *abiya* mantle over his shoulder, ran down the slopes of Tel Keimun and headed towards the grazing grounds of Sheikh Abreikh, marshy pastures near the ruins of the Moslem saint of that name's tomb. Before he reached the Israeli village of Mishmar Ha'Emek he struck up into the hills, meaning to cross them west of Megiddo, and so descend the Um el Fahm pass to reach the neighbourhood of Kuryet Jett in due course. He had to use infinite care and caution to save himself from falling into the hands of the regular Arab troops who were patrolling in a frantic search to seize the ambushers and so save their leaders' faces when the outrage was brought up at the next sitting of the United Nations. There was even greater danger from the ambushers themselves, who, cock-a-whoop with the shrewd blow they had struck at the Forgotten-of-Allah, were ready to shoot at sight anyone who tried to prevent their returning to their own homes.

Jonathan had several narrow escapes, and on at least three occasions only his perfect Arabic and ready wit saved his life. By the time dawn came he was high in the hills, and finding one of the caves with which the Mountains of Samaria are riddled, he holed up for the day, despite the fact that he had not eaten since the previous noon-day's rest among the labourers on the road.

He reckoned that he was less than a couple of miles from the main road which connects Jenin, on the southern borders of the Plain of Armageddon, with Nablus deep in its valley between the Mountains of Ebal and Gerizim, but he decided to go no nearer to it for fear of being seen by regular Arab army patrols. Far below, Jonathan saw the coastal plain, its fringe of gold marking the sands of the seashore, with the limitless purple of the Mediterranean, glinting and dancing in the sunshine far beyond. Somewhere between him and the edge of the hills lay Kuryet Jett, the village which he had come so far to seek.

He slept soundly until just after midday, and walking along a goat-track in the mountainside, drew near the large village of Attara, which lies embowered in its fruit-trees in a deep fold of the hills below the road. Everything was very much as he remembered it during his childhood, for the Israeli State did not come so far into the mountains so that the Arab peasants remained in possession just as they had done for over a thousand years. The place was overcrowded with hundreds of refugees from parts of Palestine that had been taken over by Israel. No one took any notice of the young Arab in his mountaineer clothes who walked up the steep slope between the houses, for strangers were only too common. Near the *Zawieh*, the Guest-house, he saw that some Europeans were busy at white-topped tables and recognised them as either missionaries, or Red Cross officials dealing out the relief-goods which were sent from all over the world to help the Arabs in the extremities the Arab-Hebrew wars had caused them.

The presence of these men would not have unduly attracted Jonathan's attention if, just as he was passing, one of the men, a dark, sallow-faced individual had not lifted his face from the ledger in which he was writing. With a sudden, chilling shock, he recognised one of the two men who had tried to kill him aboard *Symondsbury Mote* off Aldebaran, and again on the Dorchester Road. Jonathan shrank back into the shade of one of the houses and, squatting on his heels in the dust, as any Arab might have done, he pulled his flowing *abiya* mantle around him and settled down to watch.

A few seconds later he saw the second of the dagger-men, and shortly afterwards, the man who, wearing the American officer's uniform, had driven the big Buick into the side of the little car. Jonathan gulped but after recognising this trio, he was not unduly surprised when, to complete the party, a pock-marked Chinaman appeared, wearing a big Red Cross brassard on his arm, and he saw that it was Cheng Loo!

He could have kicked himself for having been so long in reaching this part of the world, for during the time which had elapsed since the burglary the brutes had had plenty of chance to discover that they had been led astray by the papers they stole from the Samways' home and also to double back and get on to the right trail. But how could they know where to look? Were they here by chance? Or were they waiting for him to appear and unwittingly lead them to the Red Cormorant's hiding-place? Why were they so close to Kuryet Jett? Did they know the clue which von Thurstein had left? Jonathan mentally repeated the translation of the Red Cormorant's riddle.

"Seek in the north-eastern corner of the Magus's first workshop. In the niche that he cut for the tools of his trickery I have put the paper."

Colonel Samways had solved that puzzle very quickly for his most beloved hobby during the long years he had served in the Holy Land was a study of its historical geography. He had identified many places which even George Adam Smith had missed when he was writing his wonderful book on the subject, and was considered an authority in his pet subject.

"The Magus," the Colonel had explained to Jonathan one night in West Dorset while his son sat beside his bed discussing the expedition, "to whom von Thurstein referred is probably Simon

Magus, the sorcerer who received such a scathing rebuke in '*Acts of the Apostles*,' Chapter Eight, verses 9 and 10. You may recall how he tried to offer them a big bribe to show him what he thought were the conjuring tricks by which the holy men performed their miracles."

Jonathan had sat silent while his father elaborated his theory. "Yes," he said, "I'm sure that I'm right; it is just the sort of clue that the Red Cormorant, with his wide Scriptural lore would use. Simon the Magus is supposed to have been a native of the Samaritan city of Gitto, which is the ancient name for the village we now call Kuryet Jett. Come to think of it there *is* a big cave in the hill north-east of the village which was probably a tomb, long before the days of Simon Magus which the Arabs still call the Sorcerer's Workshop. Yes, I'm convinced that Kuryet Jett is the place we want."

It all sounds flimsy enough when set down in cold print, but to a Palestine enthusiast it made sound sense, in any case it formed the foundation which sent Jonathan to Palestine. He supposed that the gangsters had picked up information that the Red Cormorant had worked in the Samaritan Hills when he was engaged in his Secret Service work against Britain in 1941 and deduced from that that Jonathan would appear somewhere in the neighbourhood. Whatever had brought them, they were in the Samaritan Hills and with a perfectly good excuse to cover their movements. As members of the Relief, they were able to glean all the information they needed about any strangers who appeared in the neighbourhood.

The more Jonathan thought over it the more he became certain that the gangsters really had deduced that the Red Cormorant had his hiding-place somewhere in the Jebel Nablus, as these hills are called, and were now awaiting his arrival to give them a direct lead. Jonathan sat wondering how he could best take advantage of this slight start he had gained, of knowing about their presence before they learned of his, and decided that it would be best to start for Kuryet Jett as any further delay might be fatal.

Cheng Loo walked away, bearing a tray of emptied tea-cups, for he was playing the part of being a servant to this section of the Relief, and, fortunately, was already inside the house when an Arab, a Nazareth Christian by his dress and manner, came to Jonathan's side, brandishing a note-book.

" By the markings of your *abiya*, O my brother," the man said oilily, " You are from the southern limits of the Plain of Armageddon. Is it for help that you have come to this village? If that is so the Franks who control the Relief will judge your request and give you help if they think your case needs it more than others; they are short of many things and so must give what little they have to the most deserving of the poor who come to them. I am their adviser in these delicate matters."

Jonathan could cheerfully have kicked the smiling rogue. The hint was broad enough that, if he cared to give the clerk a small bribe, his name would be placed well up the list of deserving cases. The gentle-faced women and the worthy men dispensing the Relief had of course no idea of the treachery of their servant.

"I am desolated, effendi," Jonathan said, humbly and hopelessly, "I fear I am destitute, so I have nothing to offer your nobility which may induce you to shine the light of your favour upon me."

"In that case," the man replied, brazen-faced, "I must seek others who are in greater need of the aid which I can advise the Franks to give."

Jonathan forced himself to carry on with his part, but he must have made an unwitting slip which half-roused the official's suspicions that the Arab lad might not be what he pretended to be. The swindling villain feared that some spy might be sent from Red Cross headquarters, where there were plenty of people who knew the shady tricks that the people whom they were forced to employ, might try. If this lad was one, the official thought, uneasily, then the sooner arrangements were made for his disappearance the better it would be.

Without any inkling that he was under suspicion, Jonathan slipped away a few minutes later between the little cube-shaped houses. He had no least reason to know that he was being studied through high-powered Zeiss glasses as he took his way down the valley through the olive-groves, nor that Cheng Loo and one of the gangsters had left the village as soon as he was out of sight.

He went more quickly along the goat-track as soon as he was out of sight of Attara, a part of the country he knew extremely well as his father had been in command of the Nablus District. He struck away down a track through the foothills towards the village of Kuryet Jett and as he was protected by his Arab clothes he could see no particular reason to wait until dark.

He met several wayfarers and on some of the higher vantage-points commanding the criss-cross of valleys, he noticed posts of regular Arab troops, mainly men of the Jordan Arab Legion who were keeping watch and ward against any incursion of either Israeli troops or irregular raiding-parties. Jonathan passed fairly close to one of them but, bar being challenged and then told to go on his way, he was not delayed by the soldiers behind the stone sangars. Then, quite suddenly, as he topped the crest of a ridge, the ground fell away towards the coastal Plain of Sharon, which, at this place is about eight miles wide, with the dark masses of the eucalyptus woods and orange-groves of long-established Jewish agricultural colonies studding it in the light of the setting sun.

Immediately below, six hundred feet down, the houses of Kuryet Jett glinted yellow-grey in the levelling beams of the westering sun crowning a knoll composed of the different cities which have stood on the site. Faint and far away he saw the white plume of steam from a locomotive drawing a train down the main line, while, somewhere in the skies to the westward was the drone of an Israeli aircraft on patrol.

Jonathan committed a foolish action by not studying his back-trail, for, if he had done so, he must have seen the three Europeans and their Chinese servant riding along on the path from the heights above before they were hidden in a grove of olive-trees close to a village. But he did not do so and went swiftly on towards Kuryet Jett, hoping to find the Cavern of the Sorcerer's Workshop before it became too dark, prior to claiming to be an innocent wayfarer with a right to hospitality in the village's *Zawieh*, as have all Sons of the Faith when on their travels.

A mile beyond the village he saw the zig-zag of earthworks marking the Israeli advance-line, which protected the plain against attacks from the threatening hills. There was a momentary flicker of bright steel as he looked towards the Hebrew lines and Jonathan guessed that it was the shine of the fixed bayonets of the Night-guard as they paraded for the night.

In the fading light Kuryet Jett, which stands, as

has been said, on a high knoll, looked like a mediaeval fortress, an illusion that was heightened by the fact that its houses are built end to end right round the crest of the steeply-rising ground and as they have few windows in their blank rears they seem like the wall of a city. But there are plenty of gaps in the wall so there are no gates that can be closed. A broad valley lies between the mountains and the knoll, and Jonathan hurried to get across this open ground before the sun sank.

He pressed on so quickly that he reached the range of ancient tombs in the hills and found the huge chamber called the Sorcerer's Workshop without Cheng Loo and his confederates seeing where he had gone. They imagined that the lad whom they were pursuing had entered the village and it was only when they dismounted that they learned from a woman who was carrying a jar of water on her head as she returned home from the well, that she had seen a man entering the devil-haunted caves beyond the base of the hill.

Jonathan was overjoyed ; he quickly discovered that his father had been perfectly correct in his calculations. He explored the recess described by von Thurstein, and inside found a small bottle, its cork covered with sealing wax. Within he could see a small twist of paper and breaking the bottle, he opened the small sheet and grunted with disappointment at what he saw. It said that he was still many hundreds of miles from the place where the Red Cormorant had hidden his Hoard.

It was at that moment that the last rays of light streaming through the narrow, square door of the ancient tomb were blotted out by a human body forcing its way in. Whipping round, Jonathan, who was standing in the furthest dark corner, saw a second man coming in while a mocking laugh spurted from the leader. Cheng Loo's well-remembered voice was speaking suavely.

" We meet again, most honourable Mister Samways ! Now that we have found the hiding-place of the treasure it is regrettably necessary to dispose of you for you are no longer of any significance. It will be easy and simple for I hold your death in my hand, and no one ever visits this dark haunt of evil fame."

Chapter 12

Footsteps on the Dark Hillside

Cheng Loo, a man who seldom erred, had made a disastrous mistake. He could not see Jonathan in the dark corner of the ancient rock-hewn sepulchre and his bluff had failed. He had taken the even chance of choosing the right direction but he was facing the opposite corner to that in which the lad was crouched, fully aware that the yellow man would whirl round at the first sound and show not the least hesitation in pulling the trigger.

Jonathan thrust the small piece of paper into his mouth before hurling himself straight at the Chinaman's knees in a flying Rugger tackle. He brought Cheng Loo crashing to the ground before he was able to face halfway round to meet the attack, so that his pistol exploded harmlessly, the bullet hitting the low roof of the sepulchre. He drove one of his soft Arab camel-skin boots, armed with its steel plates to grip the sand, on to Cheng Loo's forearm as the man fell prostrate wringing a scream of agony from him and forcing him to release the blued-steel weapon which Jonathan snatched from the floor.

Everything happened with hurricane speed,

probably not more than five seconds elapsed from the moment when Jonathan launched himself at the Chinaman's knees before the English lad was back on his feet with the pistol in his hand, its muzzle spitting fire at the two men who were trying to rush into the cave to learn what the trouble might be. One of his bullets hit the taller of the two dark-faced men and threw him back on his companion. Jonathan instantly sprang forward, ignoring Cheng Loo who was squatting on the floor behind him, dazedly nursing his sadly-bruised head which had hit the floor, and his bleeding forearm. Jonathan swallowed the paper he had been chewing and then, as he emerged from the cave, a pistol flared in the darkness sending a bullet so close to his head that he felt the burn of it on the tip of his ear as it buzzed past. Swinging his captured gun in the direction from which the flash had come he sent off a shot which brought a grunting-scream from the target as evidence that he had not missed.

Jonathan turned and ran hard down towards the valley, across the flat land at the base of the knoll, and, as he did so, a small searchlight stabbed the night from the houses of Kuryet el Jett, its beam questing towards the Sorcerer's Workshop to discover what was causing all the uproar then a machine-gun chattered for a couple of seconds. The officer in charge of the Arab Legion's advanced outposts in the village was afraid that some Israeli irregulars might have defied their own Government's orders and staged a flying raid into Arab territory as a repisal for the outrage at Tel Keimun. Bugles blew further back in the Samaritan Hills as the alert was sounded among the outposts and company-headquarters—the whole mountain country was suddenly awake and on guard.

Jonathan saw that he could not have the least chance of getting away unobserved while the alert lasted and decided that he would go to ground as quickly as he could. There were several deep ditches in the valley, dry water-courses, *wadis* is the local name, where the torrents flow from the mountains in the rainy season to the distant Mediterranean. The *wadi* he found was nine feet deep and about a dozen wide at ground level but contracting to a yard or so on the bed of white, water-worn, round pebbles which filled the bottom of the torrent's course.

The night became wildly busy. Somewhere among the hills above there was a short sharp burst of machine-gun fire as some trigger-happy Legionary fired at something he thought suspicious. Twin beams of light shone on the edge of the plain along the road from Tulkarm, the big town at the foot of the valley which comes down from the city of Nablus, as armoured-cars summoned from the town, thrust north to reinforce any threatened post, or cut off the retreat of any Israeli irregulars who might have got through.

Jonathan found a perfect refuge beneath a section of the bank which was undercut by the scurry of the rainy-season's floods. He was quite invisible to anyone who was not actually walking along the dry bed of the *wadi*, but all the same he lay very still when he heard excited shouts from the knoll on which the village stood, less than a quarter of a mile in a direct-line from his hiding-place. Two more shots rang out and then he heard Cheng Loo's scream, and this time the Chinaman was too frightened to maintain his usual impassive calm. Jonathan chuckled to himself wondering how the other two brigands, both of whom he was sure were wounded by his bullets, and the Oriental would explain their presence to the Arab soldiers—he imagined they would find it very difficult.

His amusement was very short-lived, however, for almost at once he remembered that the gang were ostensibly members of the Foreign Relief organisation : they would not find it very difficult to establish their credentials. Perhaps, too, they might set the whole of the Arab forces hunting for the " spy " whom they would claim had attacked them in the Sorcerer's Workshop when they had gone there for shelter after darkness had made it too hazardous to approach the Arab Legion's advanced outposts. Things were not so funny, he wryly reflected. Before very long hundreds of soldiers would be hunting for a European disguised in Arab clothes, and once they got hold of him it would not be long before he faced a firing-party!

The dangers from the gangsters had been bad enough, but Jonathan with a cold, sinking feeling in the region of his heart realised that he had never been in such deadly danger as he was at that moment while he crouched in the dry water-course. His only wish was to get away from Palestine as quickly as he could, for the paper he had swallowed had told him that the Hoard was hidden far away in Cyrenaica, among the hills of the Jebel Akhdar, where the Red Cormorant had buried it after the Battle of El Alamein sent the Germans reeling back, never to regain their former conquest.

White pencils were shining high in the sky over towards the sea where the Israeli frontier-guards, roused by the activity inside the Arab lines, had also manned their own posts, afraid on their own side that Arab irregulars might be trying to force their way through the Legion's area to kill and burn and harry the few villages on the plain set up since the birth of the new State. Jonathan saw the reflection of the Israeli searchlights with deep alarm as there would now be little chance for a fugitive to slip across the debatable land between the Armies standing-to at battle-stations. Anyone in Arab dress caught in one of the questing beams would be instantly riddled by machine-guns from the strong-points and blockhouses filled with vigilant Haganah troops.

Jonathan's distress was further deepened by the knowledge that he would need to move very quickly if he was to be away before the Arab Legion organised their sweep up the valley. Anything was better than staying where he was, for the *wadi* was one of the most obvious places, exactly where the troops would expect any fugitive to hide. His brain raced as he did his best to calculate what the hunters would expect him to do—if they believed that he was an Israeli spy then the natural thing for him to do would be to make a dash for his own lines—the main strength of the Arab search-lines would therefore be on the flat land at the foot of the hills. He must head, then, for the hills—up in the wild fastnesses of the Samaritan Mountains he might stand a better chance. More, the gangsters themselves, who would naturally take quite a different line from that of the soldiers, might anticipate that he would strike into the hills, but even they would not expect him to go back to their own base, Attara, the village where the Relief Unit was working. Thrusting his head right into the jaws of the trap was the least likely thing that any man fleeing for his life would do. In any case, as Jonathan consoled himself, two of the brutes were presumably knocked out so that only Cheng Loo could still be in a fit enough condition to pursue him.

The sounds of troops parading in the village were now quite unmistakable while, away beyond the brow of the southern hill the glow of head-lights filled the sky as armoured-cars and lorries crammed with troops from Tulkarm spread out to man their sectors of the cordon being formed to cut the suspected spy off from Israeli territory. Jonathan rolled out of his hiding-place, and as soon as he had done so he was strongly tempted to creep back, for it seemed so safe a place in a world that was filled with deadly and instant peril. He resisted the urge, however, and turning east, ran swiftly to the foot of the steep, rock-covered hill. He went up it with all the agility of a native shepherd boy, the long folds of his *abiya* mantle thrown back over his left shoulder in a way that the Arab hillmen affect when they wish to move fast.

The beam of the searchlight from Kuryet Jett almost caught him before he was six hundred feet up the slope ; he had no preliminary warning of the beam sweeping across the hillside, for, by sheer chance it was switched on at the very moment when its lens was directed almost directly at him. The sudden flood of blinding light dazzled him so completely that he was halted in his tracks. That probably saved him, as the soldiers on the knoll below would instantly have detected any movement made so close to the path of the incandescent sword of light. If it had been swung to the left he would have been bathed in it, but, by sheer good fortune the beam slowly traversed to the south, away to his right.

Meanwhile Jonathan, as soon as the light began to swing, dropped behind a big boulder where he lay, recovering his breath and wondering what he should do next. The light was extinguished a few minutes later after it had swept back and forth along the grey slopes, and taking full advantage of the darkness he rose to his feet and started towards the crest. He would have a better chance up on the summit to keep clear of the Arab Legion outposts covering the passes and valley-tracks.

It took nearly an hour to get to the flat ridge of the long hill, and there he paused for a while to make sure of his surroundings. Years before he had accompanied his father on a partridge-shooting expedition across these mountains, and he thought he remembered enough of the region not to get lost. He slunk along the ridge, keeping below the skyline, meaning to reach Attara well before dawn. As he walked swiftly along, he several times saw lights away below him on the plain, showing that both Arab Legion armoured-cars and Israeli frontier-patrols were still very much on the alert.

It was cool and fresh on the hill-tops with a light wind blowing in from the sea to set up a gentle soughing among the tall sun-dried grass and sparse scrub, but he saw no signs of anything human. Jackals on the slopes below him raised their thin, weird screams, sounding like women in bitter pain ; twice he heard the unearthly laughter of hyenas that resembles the evil merriment of fiends in *Jehennum*. A covey of red-legged partridges whirred up from beneath his feet as he stumbled upon them, and, at least once, he thought he had fallen into an ambush as a sharp rattle commenced close to his left. The sound brought him to an abrupt halt but as he stood, expecting the flash of a rifle, for he believed he had heard the click of rifles being cocked, he breathed again as he identified the sound as the hoofs of a couple of gazelle who darted away from this strange midnight intruder.

A few miles further along he dropped into a valley as the range on whose ridges he had been travelling, lost all further contact with the crests to the eastward. Down below him ran the road connecting Tulkarm with the Nablus-Nazareth road, with the firelights of a military outpost, placed under the arches of the ruins of a Roman aqueduct, with the steel lines of the metre-gauge railway beside it glinting faintly in the bright star-shine.

There was no way round, Jonathan saw he must cross the valley and climb the hills on the southern side, but his heart sank as he realised he could not now get back to Attara before daylight made further movement too dangerous. There was no help for it, however, and then he remembered when his father took him to see the Passover Sacrifice offered among the ruins of their temple by the Samaritans from Nablus, the last remnants of the Ten Tribes. If he could reach those ruins he should be safe for a few hours.

There were many olive trees on the lower slopes as Jonathan neared the main road, but he knew that the nearest village was a mile down towards the Plain of Sharon. The fire of the Legion's outpost at the viaduct glowed redly as one of the night-guard ground the bottom of his blackened coffee-pot into the embers, and for a moment there was enough light to show the man's form outlined against the ruddy light. Jonathan turned away along the hillside, dodging from one ancient tree-trunk to another, hoping to get further away from the sentries who were so unexpectedly alert, and as he did so he dislodged a rounded stone which rolled noisily away down the slope, dislodging other pebbles as it gathered speed. Jonathan, appalled by this untoward accident, threw himself flat behind one of the olive trees and peering round the stout trunk saw that the legionaries had been roused by the unusual noise.

" *Meen hennak ?* " roared a deep voice. " Who is there ? Come down at once or we open fire ! "

As he spoke a small searchlight fizzed for a

second, blinked twice, and then blazed on. The Arab soldiers had already located the direction of the rolling stones fairly accurately for the end of the beam struck the mountainside within thirty yards of Jonathan's hiding-place, and then began to sweep methodically back and forth. The voices of the soldiers were suddenly hushed by the peremptory command of a sergeant. Jonathan heard him say that the troops would sweep the hillside with a burst of machine-gun fire, and crouched very close, trying to press his body as tightly against the ground as he could, hoping fervently that the trunk of the sheltering tree was thick enough to stop the steel-jacketed bullets that would soon be whining all round him or screaming in ricochets from all the surrounding rocks.

Another and more cultured voice roared from the side of the road, dominating the bustle below as the men extended to bring as many weapons as possible to bear.

"Are you all mad?" the officer who had just emerged from his tent, demanded. "To start firing will not only bring reinforcements from all the posts in the hill to help us, in the belief that we are being attacked, but it will also make them think that the hunt for the spy who escaped from Kuryet Jett is at end. No, there shall be no firing blind up the hillside. Sergeant Ahmet," he went on, speaking to one of his junior officers. "Take a dozen men and find out what made that stone roll down the hill. The General-Pasha would call us a parcel of boys fresh from the infants' school if we alarmed the whole countryside by being such fools as to shoot into the dark because a pebble fell down a mountainside. Hunt well and maybe that will teach you to use common sense and not take such wild decisions."

Jonathan lay very still, relieved that his hiding-place was not to be smothered in a sleet of shining, tearing bullets, but knowing that a systematic search by the disgruntled soldiers, who would be sore and angry at being so publicly rebuked by their commanding officer, would be even more dangerous. Orders were muttered in the little camp and then he heard the Legionaries ascending the hillside, cursing violently as their boots slid on the rocks. So far as he could judge the men were spread out about ten yards apart with the centre, commanded by the enraged sergeant, almost immediately beneath him.

" Keep contact, men," Sergeant Ahmet commanded. " Leave no gaps unsearched. Challenge first and then fire, but if any of you shoot in the direction of his own comrades I'll have him sent to prison. Keep the line and there'll be no danger from our own rifles. Forward ! "

Despair flooded over Jonathan. There seemed to be no possible way that he could avoid being caught and, in the mood that the men were in, he knew that his shrift would be very short if once they caught sight of him. Their boots rattled on the rocks; once there was a false alarm away out on the left flank, when a soldier challenged and then fired, only to be savagely cursed for his jumpiness. The line was re-formed and, once again, started to climb inexorably towards the olive-tree behind which Jonathan lay, not able to think of any way out of the trap in which he lay.

CHAPTER 13

FACING A REBEL COURT-MARTIAL

THERE was no escape. If he tried to sneak away he would be bound to be heard and if he then made a dash for it, the bullets of the Legionaries would cut him down before he had gone very far. Even if, by some thousand-to-one chance, he did win clear, the field-telephones and portable radios of the Arab forces would promptly rouse the whole country against him. The only thing he could do was to remain still and bear as patiently as he could the blows and kicks that the soldiers would certainly give him as soon as they laid their hands on him, and hope that he would not be summarily executed before he was able to convince someone in authority of his identity. If he could do that some of them might remember Colonel Samways and then things might be well enough, if he discountenanced the fact that Cheng Loo would also be put back on his track. So far as he could see there was no way out of his danger and he was steeling himself to face the bullying troops when, on the right flank of the ascending line there was a shout, followed by a flurry of Arabic curses, and voices shrieking for mercy.

The sergeant shouted from the centre of the line and the answer came from the flank that two men had been discovered cowering in a half-ruined sepulchre-cave, whose rocky-roof had disintegrated so badly that the man on the extreme left flank had discerned two dark figures crouched inside it. Scarcely daring to breathe Jonathan lay dead still, with the nearest Legionary standing less than a hundred feet beneath him. The whole line had halted and the men stood quietly waiting for orders while from below came a bellow as the commandant of the post demanded to know what was happening.

"We have caught two men up here, Ismail Bey," the officer in charge of the party called back. "I've got an idea that they are a couple of the Forgotten of God, but I'll let you know in a moment."

There was a low babble of voices away on the flank, sounding surprisingly loud in the gentle wind stirring the sun-smitten dessicated grasses and shrubs, whose branches rattled like dry bones in the stillness. After a long minute or so, the muttering ceased and the sergeant called down to his chief.

"They are two escaped prisoners-of-war, Ismail Bey," he reported. "One is that Israeli officer whose description was circulated two days ago. What shall I do with them? Shoot them or bring them down?"

"Bring them down, you fool," his superior snorted. "Is not my brother Izhak a prisoner in the hands of the Forgotten of God? Will the General not allow this Jew to be exchanged for my brother in virtue of my having captured him? If a hair of the head of those prisoners is damaged, Sergeant Ahmet, I'll have your stripes."

Orders were given for the line to retire, but Jonathan lay very still until the recaptured prisoners were safely in the outpost and saw that everyone in it was busy either congratulating themselves, or questioning their captives. Certainly no one was paying much attention to the hillside above, and soon the Commandant gave the order to "Stand Down" and those not actually engaged on guard duties retired to their blankets and *lahafs*, the quilted bed-coverings which are used by the Arabs of the stone villages. Jonathan lay very still for over half-an-hour before he considered it safe to make a move, and when he did so it was with infinite caution not to dislodge any more loose pebbles.

He crossed the road successfully about half-a-mile and two bends above the camp at the aqueduct and so got himself onto the rocky spurs which form the western roots of the great mass of Mount Gerizim. Without being seen by anyone, although he narrowly missed a convoy of troop-cars bound down to Tulkarm, he climbed the swelling slopes and about two hours before sunrise reached the crest. The sister-ridge of Mount Ebal lay across the very deep and narrow valley with the tight-packed houses of the City of Nablus lying between, intersected by the main road to Jerusalem which was marked by the lights of passing vehicles. He was in the very heart of the part of Palestine which is still held by the Arabs and knew that every movement he might make would be fraught with peril.

His first intention had been to make for the ruins of the ancient Samaritan Temple and there to rest for a few hours in the hope that the pursuit might become less intense, but his plans were altered by an unforeseen occurrence. He was striding along the path when he suddenly heard a faint moan from his left and, going across, found an old man lying prostrate beneath the shelter of a large rock. He was groaning fitfully as he prayed to Allah, the Compassionate, the Merciful, that someone might chance to pass by and help him.

"What ails you, Father?" Jonathan asked as he bent over the man. "How is it that you come to be lying in pain in such a lonely spot as this?"

"*Alhamdulillah!* Thanks and Praise be to the One!" the man replied in the shaky, hoarse voice of a very old man. "Allah is Great! He has sent me aid. Young man, whoever you may be, I am Abu Taleb," and he paused, very much as if he had said that he was the Emperor of China. Jonathan's mind warned him to say nothing that might betray the disappointing fact that, so far as he could recall, he had never heard of Abu Taleb. Such an error might easily be fatal if Abu Taleb was a national figure who had come into prominence during the recent wars with the Israelis.

"Yes, Father," Jonathan replied, in a low voice, "I can see that you are the noble Abu Taleb. I recognise your voice."

"Good, then you will be glad to help me," Abu Taleb replied. "I was set on by two robbers just before sunset. They struck me down and left me for dead. Those rogues were of the Forgotten of God, for the Arabic that they spoke was broken in just the way that these people mistreat it."

"Let me carry you to some place where we can get aid, most honoured Father," Jonathan replied. "You may explain the assault to the officers who will avenge you later on, but now your hurts must be attended to."

"What sort of a fool are you?" the prostrate man gasped furiously. "To say that the officers will help Abu Taleb shows that you must be simple in your mind! Since when have the men who uphold the Law, whether that law was of the English who have gone, or the Hashimites who have come, or of the Forgotten of God, been likely to aid Abu Taleb?" And his voice sounded brittle with suspicion until it cracked off into a groan of bitter pain. "Who are you and whence come you?" the old man demanded.

A great light had dawned in Jonathan's brain while the old man was speaking. The tales about the old outlaw chieftain, Mohammed Abu Taleb, had been legends among the Arab troopers in the barracks of the Palestine Police. What Robin Hood had once been in English tales, Abu Taleb had become in the modern folk-stories of Palestine. In the early years of the British Mandate, Abu Taleb and his Bedouin warriors had fought battles with the men of the British Gendarmerie (a force long since disbanded) and later with the Palestine Police.

When Abu Taleb was known to be out on foray west of the River Jordan, traffic on the roads of Palestine practically ceased except in large convoys under the guns of heavy escorts. When Jonathan was scarcely four years old the brigand-chief had been captured in a battle north of Nazareth and, in due course, had been sentenced to serve a life-sentence in the great prison in the Crusader castle at Acre. He would have been hanged, in all probability, if some of the officers of the Palestine Police had not gone into the witness-box and given evidence of the many chivalrous acts which Abu Taleb had done in the heyday of his power and the fact that he had never killed a prisoner or injured a woman or child.

" I am Yussef ibn Musa el Araj of Beit Lubban in the north country, O honoured Father and Sheikh," Jonathan replied in the humblest of voices. " The Israeli soldiers captured my village and our people are scattered. I am seeking for work as a shepherd and hoping to find my folk if Allah is kind to me."

" Aye, you speak like a northerner," the prostrate man said. " Are you strong enough to carry me an hour's journey, for I must not be found by the soldiers when they come in the morning? My men await me near Khirbet es Samra, a village over the hill to the south."

Jonathan looked down at the old man and he was wondering what he should do. Abu Taleb must have been released, or else escaped from Acre prison during the confusion while Britain was ending her Mandate. He was still an outlaw, judging from what he had said, and Jonathan realised that it would be dangerous to be found in his company. For a moment he thought of quietly slipping away into the darkness, but common humanity forbade him to leave an injured man to take his chance of hyenas and human night-prowlers even more evil.

" I will carry you, Father," he said quietly. " I will take you to safety, although there is a reward of many hundreds of pounds for the man who brings you in."

" So you know that, do you ? " the old man snarled.

Glad that his guess had been right, for he had thought it likely that so famous a figure as the old bandit would have a heavy price on his head, Jonathan replied.

"Who does not know it, Lord Sheikh?" he said bending to lift the man, only to meet the sudden flicker of steel as a dagger shone in the hands of Abu Taleb.

"Carry me, boy, but know that if you try to betray me, or if you travel in any direction other than towards Khirbet Samra, you will die in the same moment that you do so."

"I will be honest, Father," Jonathan muttered.

"I have heard my father say that if it had not been for you he would have been dead."

That happened to be quite true for Colonel Samways often told the story of how, when he was a junior officer, he had believed he had cornered the Abu Taleb gang in a cave in Galilee close by the Wadi Hammam, where robbers have taken shelter ever since Old Testament days, only to discover that the wily old warrior had laid a clever trap, and successfully ambushed his ambushers. If it had not been for the chivalry of the Arab chief the whole police party would have been wiped out.

"I do not recall the name of Abu Arej of Beit Lubban village," Abu Taleb replied, suspiciously.

"Yet he remembered your lordship right up to the hour of his death," Jonathan replied. "There must be many hundreds whom you befriended but whose names have not remained in your memory, Father."

"That is true," the brigand muttered, but he retained his grip on the dagger. "Bear me carefully, boy, but remember I am too old a wolf to be taken lightly. If there is treachery in your heart know that it will be loosed by my dagger-point long before I am taken prisoner should you lead me into an ambush. Even if you try to drop me suddenly, I will rip out your bowels before I reach the ground."

"You may trust me, Lord and Father," Jonathan murmured and carefully carrying the old body, which he found surprisingly light, he turned towards the crest which hid Khirbet Samra, and strode away through the dry herbiage rattling in the wind. Before he had gone very far he felt his patient suddenly relax and only just caught the dagger as it dropped from the unconscious hand which could no longer hold it. Jonathan grinned, stuffed the weapon into his waist-cloth and plodded on. As he went he reflected that this was one of the luckiest things that could have happened to him, for as Cheng Loo's main strength lay in the fact that he could enlist the aid of both Arab and Israeli Governments, because of his position as a member of the Red Cross Relief Organisation, he was not likely to get much support from a band of hardy irregulars commanded by the veteran sheikh.

As he trudged along the unconscious body grew heavier and heavier, but to cut a long story as short as possible, he reached Khirbet Samra after sundry adventures. He was nearly killed by the Green Brotherhood's alert sentries as he approached the village. He delivered the injured sheikh into the capable hands of the Moslem doctor serving with this band of fanatical warriors who had pledged themselves to recognise no peace with the Israelis, so long as a single acre of Palestine land remained in their possession.

One of the long-mantled sheikhs, Abu Taleb's second-in-command, told a warrior to find the youngster a bed and some food, but said that he would not be permitted to leave the village until Abu Taleb himself had given orders regarding him.

"We cannot allow strangers to wander the land and say that they have found the Green Brotherhood in camp," he explained. "Have no fear, however, the Great Sheikh will surely reward you fittingly for all that you have done on his behalf. "Remember, however, that no matter how grateful we may be to you we shall shoot to kill if you attempt to leave us before permission to do so is given you. Be wise and take heed."

Jonathan was only too pleased to have the chance to rest in safety and as soon as he entered the small room in one of the verminous hovels from which the ordinary population of the village had fled during one of the battles of the early days of the war, he stretched himself on the long, rammed-earth shelf at one end of the room and was almost instantly asleep.

He woke, hours later, to find the room crammed with fierce-looking Arabs, every man wearing bandoliers of cartridges crossed on the breast of his grey *demiya*, the nightshirt-like garment which the hillmen wear beneath their short jackets. They had at least two pistols in their gaily coloured waist-bands as well as a modern rifle slung over their shoulders. Their brown, hawk-like faces showed beneath the folds of the green headcloths they all wore, secured to their heads by the twin black rings of their *egals* made of tightly wrapped goathair thread. A one-eyed man, who bore a livid wound on his right cheek was shaking Jonathan's shoulder while he struggled upright rubbing his eyes aghast at the sight of these fierce warriors.

"Rise, boy," the chieftain said with a rumble of menace in his steely, commanding voice. "You are to appear before the noble Sheikh Abu Taleb and if you can offer no reasonable explanation why although your skin is that of one of the Forgotten of God, you wear the clothing of a man of our race and have declared yourself to be one of our people from Galilee, I fear that you will be taken out from his presence to face a firing-squad as a spy."

Jonathan kept his face expressionless as he met

the fierce eyes of the hill-fighters. There was no sense in betraying the fear that was racking him—that could lead only to his instant despatch at the hands of these men who had suffered so greatly at the hands of men with pale skins. He rose as calmly as he could, and without a word stood submissively before them, his whole demeanour showing that he was ready to be obedient.

They formed a close ring round him, while the air of hostility, of deadly hatred seemed to grow ever more intense as they walked through the dusty lane between the little houses towards the *Zawieh*, the guest-house for pilgrims at the further end. It stood on a ledge where the hillside sloped almost precipitously down to the bed of a rocky valley, a thousand feet below. More armed men thronged the approaches to the *Zawieh* and after one glance at the smouldering hate in their dark eyes, Jonathan became quite convinced that he had reached the end of all his adventuring. Inside the house he was told to take his stand in front of a dozen men, all of them older than the warriors outside, and in their midst, sitting on a heap of pink cushions covered in white cotton edged with imitation lace, the sort of bolsters usual in the better type of Palestinian hill-farmer's house, reclined an old, white-bearded, emaciated man whose high-bridged nose and glittering eagle-like grey eyes dominated the assembly.

Abu Taleb looked up from amid his cushions

at the young man in the Arab clothes and his eyes never wavered during the whole of that long minute.

"You carried me here before sunrise," he said at last. "For that I thank you, but I must first know who and what you are," and before Jonathan could reply he held up his hand to command his silence. The eyes of the other members of his council were fixed on the lad as he stood waiting for the brigand chieftain to continue.

"It is reported to me that your skin is that of a Frank, a European. It is said by some that you may be a spy of the Forgotten of God, or of some other Frankish people who wish no good to the Sons of the Faith" (by which he meant believers in the Moslem Faith.) "Although I am deeply beholden to you for saving my life, my oath as the Head of the Green Brotherhood prohibits me from showing personal favours to the guilty. If you cannot prove that you are not a spy you must die, although I will make sure that your end is swift and as merciful as possible. I was attacked by two foreigners last night—how comes it my people ask that a third foreigner should suddenly appear to save me? Was it a plan to introduce a Frank into our secret headquarters so that he might betray us? Such a dastardly plan is possible to the Forgotten of God. Now speak, and give a truthful account of yourself. Know that we are used to liars and can discern truth when we hear it."

A deep silence fell over the concourse while Jonathan feverishly sought for some explanation which might explain his presence in their midst. He knew that it would be useless to try to deceive these men. The chances were that he would be killed in any case, so why should he not tell them the whole truth in the hope that, eventually, some rumour of his end might reach his father?

"It is a long tale, worthy Sheikh," he said. "May I crave your indulgence to tell it?"

"It is for that we wait," Abu Taleb replied.

"Firstly, Father, if I had been your enemy could I not have killed you when you became unconscious and lost your dagger?" Jonathan asked quietly.

"That point has been fully considered by the Council," Abu Taleb replied, just as quietly. "In other circumstances that would be in your favour, but as it may be that you brought me here in furtherance of a deep plot to first waylay me and then to gain our confidence by your charity, it does not help you now. Speak—and do so quickly. The odds are against you; for even if you are truly innocent but cannot convince us of your lack of guilt, you must be put to death to safeguard the secrecy of our cause. Unless you can give us convincing proof that you are not an enemy, we are not endanger the Green Brotherhood by permitting you to live. Waste no more time—either confess you are a spy of the infidels—or convince us that you are our friend."

Jonathan looked from one grave face to another and saw no pity in any of them. They were as impersonal as the features of a High Court Judge in Britain.

Outside, and in the doorway, the armed brigands suddenly stirred as the warriors craned forward to hear what story this prisoner might have to tell ; every man was a member of a self-constituted jury. Jonathan knew that his life hung by a hair ; that the scales were heavily weighted against him by the need for these outlaws to preserve at all costs the secret of their headquarters. Then, too, the subtle suggestion that he might be a partner in a fiendishly clever plot to plant a spy in their midst, strengthened by their sight of his white skin, half-convicted him before he could say a word.

He gulped, his mind temporarily a blank as it failed to find the least inspiration to help him.

" You must speak quickly or we shall begin to think that you are seeking time to concoct a plausible lie," Abu Taleb said, very slowly. Jonathan sensed the growing certainty in all their minds that he was an enemy spy. " Speak at once or face a firing-squad," the old man went on. " Your sands are swiftly running out."

Chapter 14

CYRENAICAN TREASURE-TROVE

ARABIC is an ancient and a most beautiful tongue, polished by thousands of years of use by word and pen so that, unlike our modern languages which, in comparison to its venerable age are new and rude and crude, it can express the finest and most delicate shades of meaning. There is a proverb among the Moslems that theirs is the only language which can describe the colour blue to a man blind from birth. However true that may be the Arabs venerate and love their mother-tongue and nothing gives them greater pleasure than listening to a story superbly well told by someone who is a master of the Language of the Angels of God, as they call Arabic.

Jonathan had spent his childhood in the barrack-lines of the Palestine Police and had often listened enthralled to the long and involved stories told by professional *Rawis*, strolling tale-tellers, to the Arab troopers and their families. He spoke, too, with a good accent in the admired Shami dialect and loved the ancient ways of speech. That was why the rebels listened to him for so long that day in Khirbet Samra when he began the story of his wanderings.

He said nothing at all about the Hoard, he told them only about a paper which he was to find at Kuryet Jett, but he was quite truthful about everything else that had happened to him since the evening when he encountered the Red Cormorant dying on the causeway between Port Tewfik and Suez town. He wove his story skilfully and saw the hatred and rage on the faces of his audience gradually grow less as they lost themselves, first in his artistry as a tale-teller and his command of their beloved Arabic, and then, slowly became interested in his personal experiences. When he mentioned names such as that of old Mustafa Effendi, the retired police officer who had entertained him in Suez, there was a grunt of recognition from some of the men who remembered the Egyptian inspector. The same was true when other names came into the story. Slowly, cleverly, he took them with him, spending nearly two hours in the weaving of the story, using every single bit of artistry he had learned from the *Rawis* in his childhood.

Then, at long last, he came to the finding of Abu Taleb, and with the final words to describe how the chieftain's dagger had tumbled from his unconscious hand, Jonathan fell silent, careful to add not a single word on his own behalf which might distract them from the spell which he had woven round them. He looked towards the chieftain and saw that Abu Taleb was thoughtfully drawing his fingers through his white beard.

"*Wullahi!* By Allah's Self," the old warrior swore, "but you tell a good tale. So you are British—that explains your pale skin. Now tell me, would your name be Samways?"

"I am Jonathan Samways, Father," he replied, very humbly. "I am the son of Samways Bey of the Palestine Police whom some of you may remember."

That was given a very mixed reception. One or two shouted angrily that the British officer had been the cause of their going to prison, or that he had tracked down some of their relatives who had taken the walk to the gallows in Acre prison. Jonathan quaked internally, though he preserved a bold enough front and took heart when he heard words of gratitude to the British who had once ruled them. Abu Taleb imposed silence by lifting his hand.

"When lesser men dressed in red and black gowns sat in the Courthouse in Jerusalem and would have doomed me to the shameful death of the rope, it was Samways Bey who saved me. More, he made sure that I was given as honourable treatment as was possible in the Great Prison. He came to visit me when I was nothing but a number in the books, and though he was very high in the English service and I was but a convicted criminal in their eyes, he spoke to me always as one gentleman to another. He saw to the welfare of my dead son's wife and children, too, when there were few to care for them."

Jonathan felt fresh hope and a feeling of warm gratitude to his father filled him.

" Good old Dad," he thought. " Here's proof of the old saying about the bread you cast upon the waters being returned to you."

After that all was well, especially when a couple of men who had been away on scouting duty came in at that most opportune moment and bore out what Jonathan had said about the alarm at Kuryet Jett.

" One of the foreigners who works with the Relief was found dead in the mouth of the Cave called the Sorcerer's Workshop," they reported. " A second man was accidentally shot by a Legion sentry when he failed to halt, and they have also taken a slant-eyed yellow man prisoner, saying that they hold him on suspicion of being a spy, as there was no reason for his being in their advanced lines so far from his own camp. But they are seeking everywhere for a fourth man who escaped and whom the Chinese man has denounced as a famous Israeli guerilla-captain, one of those who were in charge when our women and children were massacred at Deir Yassin in the Jerusalem Hills in the days before the English left."

That caused some faces to turn towards Jonathan, for if he was one of those murderers nothing could save him from an agonising death. Abu Taleb, however, quickly turned the situation.

"Peace, brothers," he said quietly. "Look not at the son of my old friend with hate-filled eyes all laden with suspicion. We know the identity of those murdering dogs who killed our people at Deir Yassin, do we not? Is there one of them who could speak our language as this young Englishman has done? Could one of those Children of Shaitan speak the Tongue of the Angels with the purity shown by the son of Samways Bey?"

They thought this over for a few seconds and then agreed with him and thereafter there was no trouble. The rebels kept him three days at Khirbet Samra and then Jonathan began four days of the most intense activity during which every resource of the Green Brotherhood was brought into play to smuggle him through the regular Arab Army lines, the frontier posts of the Israeli forces, across the international boundary into Syria. Before leaving Khirbet Samra Abu Taleb gave him three hundred pounds in English and Egyptian notes and refused to regard it as a loan. With the dignity of an Arab prince he said that it was a trifling gift to the son of a man whose friendship he valued.

The story of that "underground" passage through the lines of embattled troops in Palestine would fill a book by itself, but let it be enough to say that Jonathan reached Beirut in safety and once there, had no difficulty in convincing the British Consulate of his identity and in getting the necessary papers for an aircraft passage home, and it was there that he made his greatest mistake. The newspapers got hold of the story that he had been moving about in the wilder parts of Palestine and, because there was a dearth of popular news in Britain and America at the moment, a great many papers made headlines of his romantic journey, fortunately without any one of them knowing what had been the true reason for his journey.

Among those who read the accounts, and who heard a mention of them on the B.B.C. short-wave news-bulletin was Cheng Loo, who had established his identity as a member of the Relief and had returned to his camp. Within an hour he was heading for Lydda Airport, where he caught a machine which carried him to Athens, where he joined a regular air-liner bound for London Airport.

. . . . .

Mrs. Rutherford, his father's housekeeper had cooked a special dinner for the colonel and his son in honour of Mr. Jonathan's return. This was a thing she seldom did, for she believed in getting the heavy work of the house finished after the mid-day meal, with only a good tea and a light supper to follow thereafter. But there had been so much in the newspapers and on the radio about Mr. Jonathan that she gladly stretched a point for once, and one of Mrs. Rutherford's dinners was a thing for even an epicure to remember.

Thick twilight covered the peaceful West Dorset countryside as father and son sat in front of the open french-windows of the library and, without any lights inside the room to attract the moths and other night-flying creatures, talked over what had happened and what they should do to complete their mission.

"Let me get this quite straight," Colonel Samways said slowly, enjoying the excellent tobacco in his pipe. "Repeat the words of von Thurstein's note which you found at Kuryet Jett as closely as you can remember."

"'I cannot return to Derna to recover my treasures because I should be recognised by the very efficient British-officered Cyrenaican Police did I do so'," Jonathan declaimed slowly. "'I leave this note in Jett so that I shall not have to carry them on my person for my life is always in danger and I am in poor health. At any time I may fall seriously ill and then this document might fall into greedy and evil hands and the ancient parchments be held up for a great ransom. I beg you who read this to give the four rolls which form the only known copy of that lost and priceless treasure "The Book of the Prophet Iddo" to which reference is made in " *Second Chronicles*," thirteenth chapter and twenty-second verse.

" ' Give these rolls to the world, but keep from the collection of my jewellery whatsoever you will, allowing the historical jewels from the Temple at Jerusalem to be handed over to the keeping of some great Museum in Germany, Britain or America.

" ' Here are the directions : Three miles west of the town wall of Derna is a small horseshoe-shaped cove with the ruins of a small building on its south-western corner. Fifty yards to the east of the ruins is a well. Ten feet down its shaft is a small door leading into what must have been constructed as a refuge from pirates. In the north-western corner of the little room is a flagstone under which lies all my Hoard '."

A silence fell over the grass terrace beneath the open windows.

" Is that all ? " the colonel asked.

" It's as near to the actual wording as I can remember it," Jonathan replied, but a sharp hiss from his father suddenly startled him :

" Keep on talking and take no notice of whatever I may do," he said, and then aloud he went on,

" We will start for Cyrenaica as soon as we can. A private charter-plane will be the best. There is the old Italian aerodrome on the top of the Libyan Escarpment above Derna, so that it will be easy for us to get there and back."

To Jonathan's astonishment his father was

easing himself out of his chair while he was speaking and as he said the last words, he launched himself through the open french-windows and convalescent though he was, crashed straight into the honeysuckle thicket that lay to the left. Jonathan jumped to his feet and dashed out to find his father furiously engaged with a writhing, snarling figure in the depths of the sweet-smelling bush. He saw, too, the flicker of steel just in time to bring his fist into the jaw of a man who had stooped over his father to drive his deadly dagger into his ribs.

Colonel Samways' falling over a branch saved him from the first ripping stroke of the knife, while his son's whizzing upper-cut preserved him from the second. Jonathan left no room for doubt, for kicking the glinting weapon away, he snatched up the tottering form of the would-be assassin, steadied him for just long enough to send in another piledriver of a blow, and then turned to his father to find him back on his feet.

"Thanks, my boy," the colonel grunted. "Now let's get this murdering swine in and have a look at him." They picked up the prostrate figure and carried it into the living-room where they laid it on the couch, Jonathan putting the knife away as his father searched the intruder and found a .38 Colts automatic pistol in a shoulder holster.

"Switch on the light," Colonel Samways

ordered, and as Jonathan did so he gasped with sheer unbelief.

"Why, it can't be," he said in a voice that was almost a shout. "It's Cheng Loo himself."

Something in his voice must have penetrated the fogs round the Chinaman's brain, for one beady eye opened and then, quick as a darting-snake, his hand streaked for the shoulder-holster beneath his jacket.

"I've got your gun, Cheng Loo," the veteran police officer said grimly. "I'd advise you to stay quite still—the law of England still allows a man to defend his own home against burglars, so I'll incur no trouble by shooting you if you turn violent."

"What are you going to do with me?" Cheng Loo asked, and his yellow mask showed no slightest trace of fear, scarcely, indeed, any of interest. It looked as though he was discussing something which had no particular bearing on himself.

"You need not worry," Colonel Samways said, very quietly. "So long as you behave yourself you have no more to fear than a long term of imprisonment. I am sending for the police and when they come I will charge you with burglary, illegal carrying of firearms and attempt to murder me with your dagger. If all goes well you may escape with seven years in prison, if you are unlucky it may be as much as fifteen. That is all—

but if you care to keep your tongue between your teeth I will drop the charge of attempted murder, in which case you may receive as little as three years."

"That is a bargain," the yellow man replied, gravely. "I shall plead guilty to honourable judge and jury. You will say nothing about my attempt to kill you. Is it agreed?"

"It is agreed," the colonel replied just as gravely.

"The ways of Fate are indeed strange," the Chinaman went on in a sing-song philosophical voice. "I spent much money, I ran great risks, I endured much fatigue to learn the secret which I now know but cannot use. Still, that is my destined fate and as a Moslem of Mongolia I must accept what is written."

. . . . .

Thereafter matters ran smoothly. There was no difficulty in interesting the British Government in the story of the Red Cormorant's Hoard. Agreement was reached with the Emir of Cyrenaica and Jonathan, accompanied by his father, was whisked off to Derna in an R.A.F. machine. A few hours were enough to find the hoard and bring the priceless documents to light. They were far too precious to be sent home by air, and a destroyer, which was due to return to Devonport to pay off at the end of her commission, took the two Samways home and the Biblical scripts to the experts who were feverishly waiting for the little warship to berth.

THE END

Adventure Stories for Boys and Girls

With full colour frontispiece and jacket and four photographic plates.
6/- *net each.*

Challenge of the Firebrand

By ELLESTON TREVOR

A high-speed story telling how three youngsters designed, built and raced a 750 c.c. Special car against the crack drivers of the world's racing-circuits.

It is a story of back-breaking work, high courage, team-efficiency and the brilliant, inspired driving of Firebrand and the pathway it blazed from England to the Continent, from secret beginnings to final victory. A hounding, pace-wild yarn.

Tadgy on the Trail

By NELSON DAVIS

" A gripping thriller," was *The Scotsman's* verdict on the previous story about Tadgy (Plantaganet) Prance, the boy detective. " The excitement rises to tremendous heights," wrote another enthusiastic critic.

Equally exciting is this splendid new yarn of the Welsh hills in which Tadgy and his friends probe the mystery of a remote hillside farm and follow a hazardous trail to the dangerous men whom Scotland Yard are seeking.

HERBERT JENKINS, LTD., 3 Duke of York St., S.W.1.

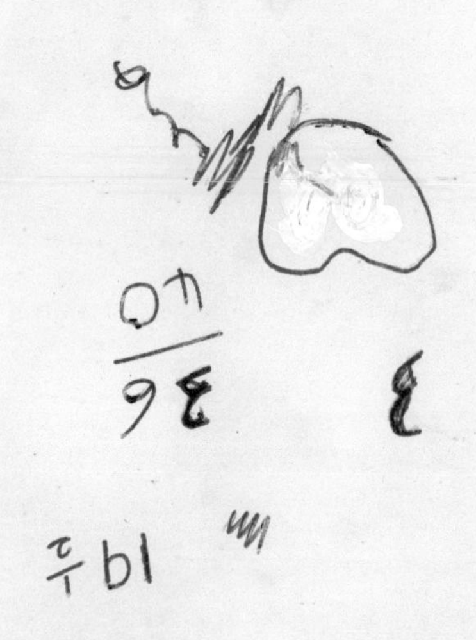